NO ESCAPE

After I put away my golf clubs, I heard the coach call: "Hurry, Rilla, the photographer is waiting."

I wondered—why a photographer for a high school golf match? Was this for our yearbook?

"Who is the photographer?" I asked Seth.

"He's from the *Ledger*."

A feeling of panic welled in me. My picture in the *newspaper?* Suppose the nurse at Longwood Hospital should read the Sunday paper and see this photograph? Would she recognize me? I started to tremble.

"Will the young lady hold her head up a bit?" the photographer said.

I wanted to shout: "I won't have my picture taken!" Maybe I could move my head just as he snapped—make myself a blur?

I forced a smile, aware only of a stupid desire to cry. Was this going to be my life from now on? Sudden alarms? I could almost picture it: afraid to go around corners, afraid to meet new people, afraid—always afraid. . . .

"Ready?" said the photographer.

Hope Dahle Jordan

HAUNTED SUMMER

AN ARCHWAY PAPERBACK
Published by POCKET BOOKS • NEW YORK

An Archway Paperback published by
POCKET BOOKS, a Simon & Schuster division of
GULF & WESTERN CORPORATION
1230 Avenue of the Americas, New York, N.Y. 10020

Published by arrangement with Lothrop, Lee & Shepard Company
Library of Congress Catalog Card Number: 67-15713

ISBN: 0-671-43871-9

First Pocket Books printing February, 1969

19 18 17 16 15 14 13

Printed in the U.S.A.

IL 7+

For our children:
Dave, Hope Claudine, Rich and Jimmy

HAUNTED
SUMMER

Chapter

:1:

If you live in Longwood and if you are a daily reader of the *Ledger* you have been reading about me lately. You probably started my story at the beginning (from the fog-shrouded April evening when a paper boy named Lyle Abbot was forced to make his deliveries very late because of the weather, and was hit by a car he never saw) but you don't know who I am.

I'm the *X* in the case. I drove the car.

Since that ghastly night I have been studying newspaper accounts of hit-and-run accidents. I've noticed that as a general rule a story runs only in one issue. Even when there's a death, which as yet is not the case with the paper boy, there is only a single write-up, and that's all.

Not so with *my* accident.

No. Because of what it termed the *pathos* of this special case (*X*'s pathos rather than the paper boy's), the *Ledger* has been running frequent stories about me. I must be a good kid, they have concluded. After all, I picked up the paper boy after the disaster. I drove him to the hospital, I saw that he got immediate attention, and I waited and waited in a bare white-tiled corridor. I waited—*oh, how I waited!*

Minutes. An hour. An eternity.

Then I panicked and I ran.

The Haunted Boy. That's the name the *Ledger* has given me.

To you, the residents of Longwood, I have become a conversation piece. I am this month's substitute for the weather. The police, via the front page, have sent me advice. "Give yourself up, son," they have warned. A symposium of high school students (some of whom I know by sight at Kennedy High) have told what they would do if they were me. Ministers of various faiths have spoken to *X* through the *Ledger*. "You run and you run, but you can never run far enough or fast enough to flee from yourself."

Recently, the state newspapers picked up my story. It had emotional appeal, I heard my father say. They even hired a psychiatrist to make a sketchy attempt to analyze me.

The very latest publicity is the biggest of all—a national weekly magazine decided that this particular hit-and-run had impact for them. To prepare it, their artist has drawn a picture of me as described by the only hospital employee who saw me. Mrs. Jones, the employee, said she was too worried about her patient to notice details. The cover shot shows me as a thin boy hunched up in a golf jacket, fingers in my hair, legs twisted around a chair. My head is turned so you can't see my face and I'm staring down a white-tiled hospital corridor that seems to stretch from here to forever.

Yes, plenty of ink has been used to tell of my hit-and-run accident. You Longwood readers must feel you know almost all there is to know about me—except my name. I am a nice, well-intentioned lad, you think. Maybe I am unaccustomed to trouble and, consequently, I was shocked into doing the wrong thing by running away. Anyway, that's the impression the *Ledger* is building about me. A scared young man. Biting his tongue for fear he'll make a slip some day.

The Haunted Boy.

Now I'll tell you the truth.

What nobody knows but me—except you now—is that I'm not a boy. I'm a haunted girl.

Chapter

: 2 :

My name is Marilla Marston but everybody calls me Rilla, except my father's wife.

I'm almost eighteen. Today is the first of May. Exactly one month since the accident.

It's been the kind of day that catches you by surprise after a solid week of rain. A day with clean air and green grass—warm, as if Nature had turned up the thermostat during the April dampness, and then had settled her attention on other business and forgotten it up there. The kind of day when, just a few years ago, nothing could keep me from rambling through the empty field and woods (now housing projects), searching out and thrilling over a scarlet tanager, or trillium, or the May apple spreading its umbrella, or just turning over a rock and watching new bug life stirring. The kind of day that, today, if I'd been free, would have sent me down the street to Lloyd's Golf Range.

But I had to work.

I *really* had to work after school today because now I'm the regular part-time helper at Mrs. Osmund's flower and gift shop, and today was no regular day. "We probably send out more corsages the afternoon of the May Day formal at Kennedy High than all the rest of the year together," Mrs. Osmund said as we loaded her secondhand panel truck for me to make the deliveries.

There aren't many jobs available for teen-agers in Longwood, and I was lucky during last Christmas vacation to get this one with Mrs. Osmund. And this is how I got it.

"Go down to the flower shop in a hurry," Seth Cone told me in the high school cafeteria one December noon. "That is, if you're still broke, and still want a job."

"You know that being broke is a way of life with me." I shoved my cookies across the table in his direction. "Do you think Mrs. Osmund would hire a girl?"

"She wants *help.*"

Seth Cone is my boy friend, I think. At least, he's a next-door neighbor, and a friend, and a boy. Also, he's the one person who regularly beats me at golf.

Although he conceals it so well that he is one of the genuinely popular people in Kennedy High, Seth is actually about as troubled a character as I am. Unlike me, he's an only child and he hates it. This is another reason I'm not certain whether or not he's my boy friend, or whether he just likes hanging around a house in which there's so much family that the house needs traffic rules.

Seth told me, "Every person Mrs. Osmund usually depends on to help her in an emergency is sick this Christmas." He finished his milk with my cookies. "Today she'll take anything she can get. Tomorrow may be different so—" He began stacking his empty dishes on the tray to carry to the return counter. "Strike, you know, whilst the iron is hot."

I concocted an excuse so that I could leave school ten minutes early, and dashed down to the large glass addition which Mrs. Osmund built on the front of the old Osmund home on Main Street when her husband died. With some fast talking, which isn't natural with me, I persuaded her to try me out on the lowliest jobs.

"*Anything,*" I said breathlessly, "I'll sweep, and clean, and mop—while you do the important things. I can even make deliveries if there's too much for Seth."

"No, only a boy can make deliveries." Mrs. Osmund pushed up her sleeves and retied her black plastic apron with its big pockets for scissors and pencils, and such. "I never heard of a delivery girl, did you?"

I shook my head. "But it would be different—it might be good advertising for you." I laughed, embarrassed. "Seth says there's never anything heavy to lift. I can drive a car, and I know all the streets in Longwood."

My eagerness must have appealed to her. Or maybe she was simply desperate. Anyway, she told me I could start work right then and there by straightening out the Christmas cards and decorations which were on display in what used to be a parlor, and by keeping an eye on them because she had the feeling that her inventory was getting low—without being paid for.

Now that I know her better, Mrs. Osmund has turned out to be one of my favorite people. At first, I thought she was suspicious and sharp-tongued and impatient, but that was because she was always so busy. She is plumpish, with thick, blond hair which usually looks as if she will comb it later. In her broad, high-cheekboned face, her lips are so tiny that they seem constantly puckered for a kiss. When she isn't rushed she's a comfortable person to be around, even though she talks all the time, without a comma or a period in the paragraphs of her chatter.

Her feet always hurt. Customers who know her don't say, "How are you?" They ask, "How are your feet?"

I'd only been talking when I offered to deliver for the shop. I was nervous—I had said the first thing that came off the top of my mind. But as it worked out, that's what finally happened. Seth had already told Mrs. Osmund that he would have to quit working for her after the Christmas rush. Orders from headquarters! His father so decreed! Seth is having trouble with grades. The senior year of high school is no time to be getting poor marks.

Up until this year he had been a good student. Now there's something troubling Seth. He can't concentrate. He doesn't talk about it but I've noticed that he laughs more than usual—a tight, nervous laugh rather than his old-time chuckle. And if a conversation with him becomes even slightly personal, he quickly turns the subject away from him and toward you by asking questions.

After Christmas, then, I helped Mrs. Osmund with inventory, sold small house plants and handkerchiefs and greeting cards, ran all the second-story and basement errands on the days that her feet hurt the most, and delivered a number of emergency orders.

I sort of oozed into being her delivery clerk.

I like it.

Longwood is an easy city for me to find my way around because I grew up while Longwood was growing up, and I know it by its old-time boundaries. The Arrowhead Courts and Appletree Circles and Walnut Lanes that wind for a couple of blocks and then become another builder's Dapple Drive and High Hill Road don't throw me for more than a few minutes' loss. Longwood sprawls. It was a town with few ordinances, little zoning, until almost overnight it became a city, but with proud old farmhouses squatting like mother hens with little chicks of cottages straggling out around them.

We, the Marstons, live in one of the mother hen houses.

But now I'll get back to today—May Day.

When I reached the shop right after school, Mrs. Osmund and the two housewives who are her part-time help, Mrs. Alice Smith and Mrs. Mae Smith (no relation) were loading the small black truck with what looked like unending stacks of square green boxes with see-through covers.

Corsages! I had been warned this would be a busy afternoon and evening for me—but *this?*

I must have made more of a face than I thought because Mrs. Osmund, in the tone of voice which means her lower extremities are afflicting her, said, "This is only the first load. We're really testing your mettle today, Rilla. It's a good thing you aren't going to the dance."

"Yes, it is." And for some reason I felt impelled to repeat what I had once explained to her. "A person can't go to late parties the night before an important match, you know. Tomorrow, for the first time, I'm one of the five regulars on the golf team when we play Division High. Up until now I've only been an alternate."

"Ummm. You play golf like no other girl in Longwood has ever played golf." Mrs. Osmund brushed some moisture from a box with her sleeve. "How do you find time for everything?"

"I don't. There's some complaining at home." I resettled a few of the boxes in the truck to be sure they would ride well. "I put first things first. I study. And I have to have this job with you to earn money to play golf."

I added eagerly, "Seth is going to practice chipping and putting with me at Lloyd's when I finish tonight. There—is this the last?" and I reached for the box she had in her hand.

"It's the last of the first load." Mrs. Osmund brushed her hands down on her apron. "And if you'll notice, I've arranged the deliveries in east to west order, from Eighty-fourth Street to Mountain Pass, so that you could end up at home for a sandwich before you tackle the second load."

"Mountain Pass?" Quickly I glanced at the last square box to see who on my street was getting the corsage and, as I suspected, it *was* Miss Eulalie Marston.

Chapter
:3:

The panel truck has a stick shift. Disturbed, I ground the gears as I sped away from the shop, and I hoped Mrs. Osmund was not listening. One of the reasons she's kept me at this job is her faith in my driving. She claims the truck's life will be considerably stretched with me nursing it along.

I was wishing that the last box would fall out and get lost. My sister—going to a high school dance. "I bet she'll be the only college girl there," I told myself morosely. And while I was making the first of the deliveries I wasn't nearly as polite to the customers as I should have been because, in my mind's eye, I kept seeing what the contrast would be tonight in the Marston home: me, in my old jersey shirt and jeans, and Eukie in her seafoam-green formal, looking deceptively fragile, as always.

There are several facts about our family that I ought to mention right away. It's necessary that you know about our house—and the family in it—to understand about me.

It's a special kind of house. And my parents are a special kind, too. They both have been married twice. My real mother died when I was a baby. Her name was Marilla, and she was a Johanson—the family which originally settled and formed a good portion of what is now the extreme west end of Longwood. So the house we live in is an old one because it was built when the Johansons prospered. Despite all the changes in our family, it is still called the "old Johanson place."

My father, James Christopher Marston, commonly known as Chris, remarried when I was about three. I suppose people said it was a good marriage: a widower with one daughter marrying a widow with one daughter. I suppose they patted me on the head: "Poor little tyke. A man can't raise a daughter alone. Now she's got a mother."

And later: "How nice—twins! *Boys*—along with the two girls."

So these are the people who live in the old Johanson house. My father and his wife; Eulalie, two years older than me; and Jeffrey and James (Jimbo), identical twins eight years younger than me. I'm in the middle, the step or the half sister.

Although I am often of two minds about the people living in the old Johanson place, I have only one feeling about the house itself. That is, a warm attachment which is almost a passion. Nobody would think of building anything like it today. It's a large, white structure with porches, and dormers, and a widow's walk. A Teddy Roosevelt house. It has high ceilings, wide hallways that are sitting rooms upstairs, a butler's pantry, and a full basement with a dark mysterious storm cellar. It's a house where you can stretch your elbows without bumping a wall. You can even get lost. It has a book-lined den, and a sweeping staircase which curves around a crystal chandelier that causes more "oh's" than a Christmas tree.

Best of all is the attic. *My* attic!

I was thinking about it tonight while I delivered corsages, and I could hardly wait until I finished my deliveries and would be free to go up there. I pulled up in front of the Mountain Pass Apartments where I had three stops to make. Mountain Pass makes it sound as if we've got a mountain in Longwood. Really, it's just a high hill that keeps the sun from striking the old Johanson home until nearly ten o'clock in the morning. The heights are wooded and if you can't recognize poison ivy you'd better stay clear of them.

212. The door of the apartment swung open. "Hi, Rilla." Anita Valencia's smile broadened into a grin. She seized the box I handed her. "Gee, I'd begun to think Tony had forgotten."

I don't know Anita well because her main interest is music—the Band, the A Cappella Choir, and the Mixed Chorus—but she's always pleasant even when she's scurrying along the high school corridors as if a thirty-hour day would be too short for her.

"Have a good time tonight," I said.

"You too," she sang out.

"Sure—with my golf clubs."

"Aren't you going to the dance . . . oh, that's right!" Now she looked at me with full attention. "I heard about you playing on the boys' team tomorrow—"

"It isn't the boys' team! It's the school's golf team and I had to win my way."

"I know, but . . . gee! I'll bet the guy who has to play you tomorrow will feel funny!"

I shrugged. "He'll feel funnier when I beat him."

Anita opened her mouth, but she couldn't find the words she wanted, so she shrugged too, with a laugh.

I delivered the final orders and started toward home with Eukie's box. Mountain Pass is a neat-looking street; it is lined with the most symmetrical of all trees, the maple. In the abundance of leaves live an abundance of birds and at this time of the evening they were filling the air with their bubbling, ecstatic song.

Parking the truck, I glanced up at the windows of the cupola on our house where I have my private retreat, and where I intended to take my sandwich and milk so that I could have a moment for a secret job before going back for the second load.

Odd! Was that a light that just went out up there? Couldn't be—nobody except me was allowed up there where my *real* mother's possessions were stored. True, there was no lock on the door of any room in our house; there used to be keys, but they are all lost. Yet not in years had any person except me entered my cupola. This was an *absolute.*

I looked toward the Cone house to the east of us and, for a moment, I felt like running over there to tell Seth that I still had another load of May Day orders to deliver before we could practice. But his room was dark. Probably he was trying out his new putter over at Lloyd's. The golf range, to the west of our acre of ground and just beyond Longwood's city limits, was already lighted for the customers who always carried their clubs in their cars so they could shoot a bucket of balls on their way home after office hours.

The Chinese wind harp which hangs from the ceiling of our front porch tinkled as I ran up the steps and went into the kitchen.

"Hello, Marilla." Mother was standing at the sink, cleaning celery. She has an exceptionally nice voice, so that even when she gives orders or complains it never bothers you. "Don't spoil your appetite," she said when I opened the refrigerator to get the makings for my sandwich. "We're eating early. Everybody's going out tonight."

"I have to snack in a hurry." Shoving Eukie's box along the counter, I explained that I still had more orders to deliver. "If that's wild rice in the casserole," I said, hunching my shoulder toward the oven, "save some for me, please." Averting my face from her, I asked, "Has the evening paper come?"

"It's right here on the table."

Instantly I wanted to rush up to the third floor with the *Ledger* and pore over it where nobody could watch me.

Instead, acting as if I had nothing on my mind but my sandwich, I sliced the cold meat loaf from last night's dinner, ladled corn relish on it, and put it between rye slices. I poured a big glass of milk, and automatically searched for a chocolate cookie because, as everybody in the family knows, Rilla has to have at least one bite of *something* chocolate to end every meal. It's like "amen" on a prayer.

When I glanced at Mother, I saw that she was watching me with that quiet expression she has. She is a thin, rather tall woman. Her face is not severe but her smile comes slowly; however, when it does come, it's such a complete smile that her hazel eyes crinkle nearly shut.

She was not smiling now. "I wish you'd quit that job. I don't mind the delivering, even though no other girl does that, but it's . . ." She hesitated, then continued with a sigh, "These days you're too . . . too tense and tired. I'm afraid you're trying to do too much."

"I need the money."

"I know." Turning on the faucet, she swished

the celery about in water. "With Eukie in college, even though she commutes to the city and lives at home, and with you planning to go next year, I must be out of my mind to even suggest that you leave Mrs. Osmund's, but . . ."

Again she hesitated, and her eyes on me were so searching that I felt an urgent need to divert her attention. I nodded toward the corsage box. "Is Eukie really going to the dance?"

"Why not? She's only been out of high school one year."

"Who's she going with?"

"Gaar Paulson."

"Oh, a teacher. Well—that's better." I put down my tray squarely on top of the *Ledger*. Pretending I was searching for more food, I opened the refrigerator and looked in blankly. Now I would pick up the newspaper along with my tray, and it wouldn't be obvious that I wanted it more than my food. These days I was going to great trouble to give the impression that the only thing I read in the paper were the funnies and the golf scores. I dreaded the daily *Ledger;* yet I could hardly wait for it each afternoon.

I slammed the refrigerator door. "I've got to hurry. Thank heavens there's only one May Day."

I was crossing the kitchen to pick up my tray when Eukie came sauntering in. She was already dressed for the dance. Eukie is small-boned, with a delicate feathery look as if she would catch cold easily. She has clear blue eyes, yellow hair, and a tendency to pout. But she looked especially pretty in pale green with matching slippers.

Then I noticed the long string of carved-ivory beads she was casually twirling . . . *mine.*

My mother's!

Eukie had invaded my privacy. She *had* been in my cupola. To find that rope of beads, she'd had to paw through the numerous boxes in the first drawer of the old desk. Boxes that had been my mother's and held her jewelry and trinkets that Dad had given me.

Had she searched in the second drawer of the desk, too?

Panic began to dart around inside me; I was like a fly in a window with a swatter chasing it. I had to put down my tray again or I would have dropped it. "You have no right," I began, then gulped as I made an effort to keep my voice somewhere near a normal tone. "Eukie Marston, give those to me!"

Eukie twirled, swinging her skirts and the beads. She ended, facing me. Her eyes were a cross between wide-eyed innocence and impudence. As Seth put it one day when he was annoyed with her (Eukie *does* annoy others, it isn't only me), "She wears her eyes too darned wide open."

Tossing her head, she said, "Don't you feel these beads give just the right effect, Mama?" When she knows she's about to be put on the defensive,

Eukie is quick to attack first. She gains strategic advantage; puts *you* on the defensive. "Don't you think Rilla is stingy with her old things up in the attic? She doesn't use them. Why should they just be wasted?"

I could feel my self-control cracking. I said, on a deep breath, "Give them to me!"

She sort of hugged herself. "I will—tomorrow."

I felt the blood rushing to my face and heard a ringing in my ears. A trembling seized my whole body. I shut my eyes and began to count slowly to myself. "Five—six—seven—"

"Give those beads to Rilla," I heard Mother say.

But Eukie persisted, "Mama, why do you let her get away with such selfishness? You cater to her. Maybe it's because she isn't your real daughter, and you . . ."

Mother said brusquely, "Those beads are Rilla's property. They are not to be touched without her permission."

As is customary with Eukie, she steered the argument around to her advantage: *my* selfishness, not her invasion of my privacy. Then she began a lecture on what she had learned in one of her college courses about our present child-centered culture, and about how she couldn't help but feel that Mother, completely unknown to herself, had entered a popularity contest as far as I was concerned.

With the other three children, all her own, she was not permissive. But with me . . .

With a swift movement Mother lifted the necklace from Eukie's neck, dropped it on the tray, then shoved the tray into my hands and me toward the door.

"Eulalie, there are times when you are impossible!" I heard her say as I ran up the circular staircase and dashed across the wide upper hallway to the attic steps.

The huge central room which runs the length of the attic was finished originally so that it could be lived in in all except bitter weather. Now it's our overflow room. Two old big beds with high mahogany backboards almost fill the east end. Chests and bookcases of all sizes line the walls, and above and around them hang large pictures that had served their time downstairs but that are too good to throw away—mostly because of the handsome frames.

Some out-of-style porch furniture and our former dining set makes the west end of the big room a comfortable rainy day hangout. Mother sews here. Her machine, always open, stands near the windows. Generally there's a pile of stuff to be mended on the dining table. A long mirror sits on the floor, conveniently placed for a full-length view if you are making a dress or straightening a hem.

Now, in the dimness, I encountered myself in it.

It showed a view of a young person in faded blue jeans, clutching a tray as if it were a piece of armor. I stared.

Inclining my head to one side, then the other, I studied my hair in the mirror. Had it grown at all these last few weeks? Imagine, I used to complain about how often it needed cutting! *Tawny* is the word for me—my hair, my coloring, my eyes—although Seth says I have green eyes. My face is oval. I'm not a smiler. I try to be, but I'm not. I'm taller than the average girl and I have wide shoulders, which makes my waistline look incredibly small.

"Grow—grow—" I pled with my hair, talking half-aloud, a habit when alone up there.

I saw this person in the mirror place a tray on the table with deliberate preciseness. I saw her raise her hands and press them against her temple. I saw her give a convulsive jerk to her shoulders, grab hold of her hair and pull at it, as if she'd *make* it grow longer in a hurry.

I saw a haunted girl, and then I lost her, for I turned away and flung myself down on one of the old dining room chairs. Closing my eyes, I fingered the ivory beads. I yearned for my mother who used to wear them and whom I never had a chance to know or love. I've spent hours up in this attic, fingering her possessions, touching, caressing—hoping to coax her presence to me through them.

For some moments I sat hunched over, easing my mood back into something I could handle.

Eukie. How she could throw me! Why couldn't I build some inner stronghold to protect myself from her heckling?

I've tried. I've sat here, at this table, desperately making lists of good things about Eulalie Brown Marston. When I've been sick in my fourteen years as her sister (and I've been sick a lot despite my healthy appearance and my outdoor life), she's the member of the family who'd read to me for hours when the doctor ordered a complete rest for my eyes.

Last Christmas she knit me the most beautiful white sweater I'll ever own. She likes to mess around in the kitchen—and Mother says that's the exact word to describe what she does to the kitchen—but she's the person who sees to it that there's always chocolate something-or-other for me.

She can be sharp-tongued, yes, but at the same time she has a pixie sense of humor. She's furnished me with the best laughs I've ever had. In fairness, I'd say that she jibes at herself more than at others. So I might as well admit it. The real reason Eukie rubs me the wrong way so much is I'm jealous of her.

I raised the glass of milk and sipped it slowly. I had lost all appetite for the sandwich.

Pushing aside the tray, I looked for the *Ledger*. It wasn't there. Due to the commotion in the kitchen, I'd left it downstairs. "But I've got to see what's happening!"

There. In a flash I was foaming over again because of Eukie. *She* was the reason. Since the accident I wanted to blame Eukie for everything.

Chapter

: 4 :

"Rilla—at last!" Mrs. Osmund was standing in the rear door of her shop, watching for me. This May Day rush was beginning to get her down, too. "Did you have trouble?"

I shook my head. For some reason I was exhausted. I dreaded having to make this last run of deliveries.

We began loading.

Mrs. Osmund chattered as she worked. "Nervous about tomorrow, eh? Well, that will teach you to stay out of boys' sports. Although I guess you can't call golf a boy's game these days any more than a girl's. I remember when I was young—it was a rich man's pleasure. Now *everybody* is hacking away at it.

"That's about it—except for this plant." Mrs. Osmund handed me a tall, green-papered package, the heaviest order of the evening. "It goes to the hospital."

I gulped. "Longwood Hospital?"

"Where else? To that boy—you know, the paper

boy the newspapers are writing about almost every day."

It was silly to stand there with my mouth open, but I had an odd feeling that this couldn't be happening to me. I swayed and caught hold of the car's door.

"What's the matter, Rilla?"

"Nothing, nothing at all." I practically dove into the front seat. Blindly I fumbled along the dashboard for the key, then realized that even here, out of habit, I had slipped it in my pocket as I do at every stop.

In almost complete oblivion I delivered the remainder of the corsages, arranging the run so that I would finish at the hospital. As long as possible I delayed the moment when I would have to enter Longwood Hospital, the building I hadn't been near since the night I'd fled from it. Who would receive this plant? Would I be recognized? Had my hair grown enough to alter my appearance?

The last three years, until this past month, I've cut my natural curls close to my head. My coiffure has been strictly homemade with one purpose in mind: to keep my hair out of my eyes when I'm concentrating on a golf ball.

At first Dad objected. But lately I've overheard him tell Mother that more girls ought to try Rilla's neat style, especially if their heads are well shaped.

The truck finally was empty except for the tall plant wrapped so completely I couldn't even see what variety it was. Slowly I drove to the red-brick building, insensible to the fact that I was really in a hurry tonight.

In the block before reaching the hospital I parked in the dimness under the maple trees. Drawing the plant to a spot beside me on the seat, I examined the card stapled to the green wrapping paper.

Who was sending this? Why had it been ordered from Mrs. Osmund's shop? We're just a neighborhood place with a small inventory: plants for housewives, an emergency shop for husbands remembering birthdays—corsages, and such. Was it a trap?

Lyle Abbot.

I studied the writing on the card, trying to make something out of it but, of course, it was Mrs. Osmund's. I fingered the small white envelope. It was sealed.

I don't know how long I sat there. It was completely dark. Finally I forced myself to drive the small truck around to the lower side of the hospital where, at this hour, I had to ring a bell to make this special delivery.

Through the door's pane I watched the empty basement corridor. At last a woman came around a far corner. She was large, moved heavily, and when she opened the door she was cross. "If you can't get here in time—" she began, then broke off. "Oh, I thought it was the newsboy. He's late again," she grumbled, hardly looking at me. Pointing at the plant, and to a door down the hall, she said, "Put it in the flower room—and be sure you shut the door tightly when you go out."

Nodding silently, I ducked my head and slipped away from her.

When I returned to the truck my knees were trembling. I bowed my head on the wheel. And sitting there in the truck, there was no way to prevent it: I had to relive the days I've tried to run from—that I've tried to forget, but cannot.

Chapter

: 5 :

We'd had a March of fierce winds and there is something about windy weather that puts me on edge. Thunder and lightning exhilarate me, but winds unsettle me.

I'd counted on March to get my golf game in shape because I had vowed I was going to make the Kennedy High team before I graduated. The first girl to do it.

It was a Sunday afternoon in March when Seth and I were standing in the shelter of Lloyd's boarded-up shanty of an office . . . it would be opened for business the following week. The practice field looked bleak and scraggly.

We'd both put in a couple of hours of studying this afternoon, and I was the one who had whistled for Seth to come out and get some air.

Looking up at him now, I'd say Seth Cone is genuinely handsome. Yet he has a nose that meanders a bit at the bridge because it was broken once in football, and again, by a flyball that he lost in the sun. He has prominent cheekbones in a long, thin face. So it isn't his features. No, it's his coloring that makes him handsome. He has thick brown hair which doesn't streak in the summer's sun, eyes of bitter-chocolate brown, and heavy eyebrows. Then, contrasting, is his wide, wide smile showing his good, even white teeth.

Seth has square and powerfully muscled hands and is an under-the-breath whistler when he is disturbed, unhappy, pressed or tired.

He is probably the only person who fully understands how I'm using the character-building sport of golf as a sort of improvement program on Marilla Marston. Golf is a loner's game. It's you versus yourself more than it's you against an opponent. It builds self-control and, personally, I feel I can use a lot more of that particular item.

"I wish I could put in some practice today," I said.

"It's too windy. You know what the wind does to the balls."

"But I've got to practice. Oh, Seth, you *know* how important it is to me."

"What I know is this," Seth said in an impatient voice. "You are making too much out of winning a spot on a high school team. Especially golf. It's probably the least important sport at Kennedy."

"But it's important to me!" I exclaimed and I felt tears come to my eyes. I turned around abruptly and said, "Let's go home."

So March was difficult because of the wind. And because of Seth's puzzling mood.

April the first.

Br-r-ring. My alarm rang at the early hour that was becoming routine with me ever since Lloyd reopened the golf range for the season. I washed, dressed, and drank a glass of milk before hurrying along Mountain Pass to what golfers call the Rockpile. Each morning before doing anything else and getting tired, I try to drive a bucket of balls. At night I can practice the short game, even if I'm weary.

This morning, maybe I was conscious that it was unusually dark, maybe not—I can't remember—but I certainly was not happy when I discovered the place wasn't yet open. Lloyd is generally an exceptionally early riser. I waited around, wondering if he were sick. Time was passing, and the balls were locked away from me. Fretting, I stared out at the corners of the field at the fog which obscured the far fence.

Suddenly I shivered. How eerie!

It crossed my mind that nothing seemed quite right. The amount of light. No noises. Few cars. And no golf pro.

I ran home. The house was still absolutely quiet. For the first time I looked at the clock. No wonder everyone was still asleep! It was still over an hour before my alarm should have rung.

Then I remembered that when I'd come out of the bathroom last night, ready for bed, I had bumped into Jimbo tiptoeing out of my bedroom.

"Hey, what've you been doing?"

"Just thought I heard a funny noise in there." And he'd retreated hastily down the hallway.

Now I raced upstairs, grabbed my clock and, sure enough, someone had tampered with the setting. And there was a scrawled note from the boys. *April Fool.*

"Don't blow your stack," I muttered to myself and lay down for another hour. I didn't feel like going back to practice this morning.

After school I helped clean the greeting card room. We took down and boxed the display of Easter cards. I mopped the floor, which was usually my last chore, and I was ready to hurry home when Mrs. Osmund said I'd have to go to the downtown post office with some late mail and a big package, she couldn't do the job herself because she had to dress and rush to a business banquet.

"Take the truck home from the post office," she said, noting the disappointed expression on my face. "Bring it back any time tonight when it's convenient. Park it by the back door, and put the key in the milk box."

She meant to be kind, but she had taken away my last chance of the day to work in any practice. I had to drive carefully to the post office. The fog was still pressing down, and at this time of the evening the lights of cars caught in it and looked like moons through the clouds. I tried to hurry but this simply added to my frustration.

When I finally parked the truck in front of our house and was getting out of the seat I became aware of Seth darting into his house. I didn't know what direction he had come from. But I did know that he couldn't help seeing me there, and he hadn't so much as a passing "Hi" for me.

What had come over him lately?

I stared at his tall figure disappearing through the door. Was he ashamed of me—the delivery girl? Was I too different from the other Kennedy High girls in my interests, my appearance, my job, everything?

Granted, Seth and I never talked about ourselves as steadies. But we were a combination that others had grown used to, and if Seth had found a new interest it might be hard for him, living right next door to me.

I dragged myself up the porch steps and into the house. "Oh, there you are, Marilla," Mother said with a rush. "I thought one of you girls would never come. There's a church supper tonight and they don't have enough help. So when my Circle chairman called, I told her I'd go if one of my daughters arrived home to look after our dinner. It's ready to serve but I can't trust the boys with it. Stir the gravy, will you? Don't let it burn." She slipped into her coat and grabbed her purse. "Tell Dad where I am."

I heard the door close after her. I went into the kitchen and glared at the gravy. From upstairs came the sound of the boys' feet. As long as they stayed out of my way I'd stay out of theirs.

Alone, with no prying eyes to wonder, I went

into the dark back entry where there's a window which faces across the lawn to the Cone home. I stood and stared.

Lost in thought, the next thing I knew, there was Eukie watching me.

"What are you doing?" she asked, with a tiny smile.

"Just . . . ah . . ." I cleared my throat. "Studying the fog," I said and hurried to the stove and began stirring the gravy. "I didn't hear you come in," I muttered, and hoping to divert her completely from the subject of me, I told her, "Now you can watch the dinner and the boys, and I'll take the truck back to Osmund's."

She said flatly, "I don't intend to watch the dinner, and I don't intend to watch the boys." She didn't flicker an eyelash. "That pleasure is all yours." With a swing of her skirt she left me and disappeared up the circular staircase to her bedroom.

Then—a piercing shriek from Eukie. Next, such hubbub overhead that I cringed, half-expecting the ceiling to crash on my head.

With no parent in the house to enforce order I didn't know what to do. Well, it was none of my business. "I'll just stay out of this," I told myself. "They've probably played an April Fools' joke on her, too."

A riot raged back and forth overhead. I listened, and stayed below. I was curious, but not *that* curious.

"I know when I'm well off," I was congratulating myself when Eukie came storming into the kitchen, her face scarlet, her wide blue eyes glaring at me. "It's your fault," she screamed. "You were supposed to watch them. They . . . they . . ." and momentarily she was so outraged that her words caught in her throat. "They painted mustaches with my *lipstick*—on my pictures!"

Oh! I could just see it! Eukie's dressing table, the round mirror above it ringed by class photos and snapshots of her friends, and she had a lot of them. Really, it was sort of humorous to think of cherubic-faced Gaar Paulson trimmed with lipstick, but I managed to keep from smiling.

"That's too bad—" I began.

"Too bad?" Her voice hit a shrill note of outrage. "Is that all you've got to say? Where were *you?* Why weren't you keeping your eyes on them? Mooning out the window—is that the way you mind the boys? It's your fault."

"Don't be ridiculous," I said, taking a deep breath to steady myself. There, it was happening again! Eukie was twisting the facts to fit her own purpose. There's a term in cards I've heard my parents use: "Well, you *euchred* me out of that," and every time I hear them say that word I think of Eukie and her tactics. What an appropriate word for her! That's exactly what she was doing now: euchring me into a false position.

I had to lay down the gravy spoon and stand still to hold myself steady. I would *not* lose my temper.

But I could feel my cheeks grow warm. "I was only instructed to see that the gravy did not burn —until you came home. I've done that. Now I'm taking the truck back to Osmund's. Good-bye!"

I slammed out the front door.

For a moment the old truck wouldn't start. It's like a baby: if it feels that mama is nervous and upset, it gets upset too. I pushed in the choke. I'd probably flooded it.

Finally the engine caught and I flicked on the lights. Mechanically I started along Mountain Pass.

Wow! I jammed on the brakes. A car had approached along Mountain Pass and I couldn't see it until we almost hit. My, the fog! If only I'd been paying attention before I left home, I doubt whether I would have returned the truck tonight.

Rolling down the window, I stuck out my head. If it hadn't been for the white center line I couldn't have followed the road. Well, there was no use turning back now. A good thing there wasn't much traffic!

I stared so hard at the center line, my eyes felt pulled out of my head, and I didn't even realize that I was some blocks past where I should have turned off Mountain Pass until I dimly saw the *Dead End* sign.

That meant edging the car around. Cautiously I maneuvered. I retraced my way, eyes again on the white line—and then it happened.

There was a thud and a scraping, metallic sound.

I jammed on the brakes. I didn't know what to do.

Back up? But I couldn't see!

Cold dew came out on my forehead. I was almost crazy with fear. Pumping up my courage, I pushed myself out of the car and circled the front. My immediate reaction was relief; both lights were still burning. Whatever I'd bumped—well, it couldn't be serious.

Then I saw someone lying on the pavement: a body was sprawled across a bike which straddled the curb.

A black dread washed over me but I stooped and felt for the face. There was breathing. There was a movement inside the leather jacket.

I gulped. "Can you . . . are you . . . ?"

He made a sound. It was nothing more than a faint moan.

My throat worked. The words I pushed out didn't sound like my own. "I've got to get help."

Frantically I looked around. There was nothing in the world to be seen except what the lights of the truck feebly exposed. Nothing but fog.

"I've got to get you in my car," I said gruffly, not knowing if I were heard or not. "I'll take you to the hospital." I grunted as I lifted. Thank heavens, I was tall and strong. "If I hurt you, I'm sorry."

In the back of my mind were the instructions I'd learned about accidents: don't move the victim unnecessarily. Stay at the scene of the accident. Notify police.

But in this case, in this fog—

"Somebody else could bump into us," I whimpered to myself. "I can't just stay here and wait. And I can't leave him."

He was about the size of Jimbo. Finally I got him in the front seat. He sagged against the door, which I locked so that he wouldn't fall out. Before getting behind the wheel, I moved the bike onto the lawn. It seemed a total wreck, but you never know.

That ride to the hospital—I can't recall an inch of it. It's a miracle that we got there without another accident. I remember thinking: "I ought to take him to the emergency door. But where is it?" I didn't want to search around, wasting time. Oh—by the service entrance where I'd delivered orders!

In a daze I rang the doorbell marked *Emergency.* Pressing my face against the pane, I waited.

Then I saw a woman in white coming down the long corridor. With all the strength of my golfing muscles, I half carried and half dragged the hurt boy from the truck to the door. Now the woman was looking out. "Oh, here," she cried, grabbing a wheel chair which was near the door. "Gently, gently." As she started wheeling the boy down the corridor she said over her shoulder, "What happened?"

"He . . . he was hit by a car," I gasped hoarsely.

I followed her along the corridor. At the far end were some straight-back chairs. "Wait here," said the woman as she wheeled the patient into a big elevator.

Suddenly I had a thought. *I could run. I could run*. But I waited.

I could see into a tan-tiled room divided by white curtains into small cubicles. In each cubicle was a treatment table or cart. Everything was weirdly bright from overhead fluorescent lights.

I waited. The area where I sat was hushed. It was garish with light, yet I had the crazy feeling that some of the fog had sifted in from the outside to settle in the far corners.

I waited. I can't begin to tell the strange thoughts that twisted through my mind, one starting before the preceding worry developed fully.

How badly was he hurt? Was he unconscious? I wondered who he was and then I began to wonder about his family . . . were they watching for him now, waiting dinner until he came home to eat?

His bike? Was it a complete wreck? "I'll have to make good on that," I told myself.

I shifted uneasily on the hard chair. If only I had someone to talk to! Why didn't they come and tell me something about him?

What a long, nightmarish day! Impossible to believe this was still the same April the first which had begun eons ago when Jimbo advanced my alarm setting. I was exhausted.

As I sat there waiting I had one comfort, and one alone. I *had* been watching the road, as much as I could see of it in the fog. I *had* been driving carefully. This accident had *not* happened because of carelessness.

At last!

I sprang up from the chair. The same woman who had met me at the door was hurrying down the corridor toward me. Frightened, I kept my eyes on her white shoes. She walked right by me toward an office, saying as she passed, "Follow me. We must notify his family. Would you know if there's hospitalization?"

"I . . . I don't know who he is."

"Oh dear," she said. She made a clucking sound with her tongue. "Just a minute, I'll be right back," and again I was alone.

Now I had another worry. *Hospitalization.* The expense for a new bike—that would be a blow. But hospitalization? What if his family didn't have any? Who'd have to pay? Dad? Why, his drugstore was gasping now, giving its all to support the big, old house and the large family in that house.

The store had been a thriving business when Dad had taken it over from his father, but neighborhoods change and an expressway which blocked off the streets toward the east didn't help. When our oil furnace balks, it's a cause for concern, not only because of the lack of heat. We don't own a dryer. We don't have a dishwasher, or a modern lawn mower, and Dad calls our car Methuselah.

Hospitalization—or a lawsuit?

I jumped to my feet. I couldn't stand my thoughts.

It was chilly in the corridor, or perhaps it was my exhaustion and my fear which chilled me.

Why didn't that woman come back and tell me something? Had she called the police?

I began to pace the floor, hugging myself, rubbing my arms. Then I thought about the truck. Had I gotten Mrs. Osmund into trouble? Would she be sued too?

Why didn't *someone* come?

Abstractedly, not really aware of what I was doing, I walked to the far door and looked out. I couldn't make out the corners of the parking area. In the fog I could barely see the front end of the truck.

"If she doesn't come by the time I count to ten . . ." I muttered half-aloud.

I counted to ten, slowly. I waited. I counted to twenty. Well, I would just go outside and examine the front fender. "Then I'll come back," I promised myself.

I hurried across the asphalt. With fumbling fingers I felt along the roughness of the front fender. It was old. There were many dents and scratches. But I couldn't tell if tonight's accident had added any more.

I'd have to turn on the lights.

So there I was, halfway in the front seat, reaching for the lights. The key was in the ignition lock where I'd left it when I brought the boy into the hospital.

I turned it.

Chapter
: 6 :

I parked the panel truck by Mrs. Osmund's back door and put the key in her milk box. Then I walked home, that never to be forgotten April Fools' night.

Quietly I entered the house and dragged myself up the circular staircase. Mother called from the kitchen—she'd saved supper; it was on the stove.

I didn't answer.

Up on the third floor is a hoop-backed rocking chair that my real mother had used before I was born. I went straight to it for comfort.

Tomorrow I would go back to the hospital but right now I was filled with a pain that was curious because mixed with the agony was such a large dose of numbness that it was strange that I felt anything at all.

With dry, burning eyes, I sat in the dark and rocked, rocked, and rocked.

Would the boy die? He must be badly hurt; he'd never spoken. Shuddering, I scrubbed my hands hard against my faded blue jeans.

I lost track of the time. What seemed hours later I heard footsteps. My heartbeat quickened.

Had they come for me?

I watched the dark spot where the door to the stairway should be with dull eyes. It was Dad.

"Rilla?" He snapped on the light at the head of the stairs, but we were still in gloom because we only keep 40-watt bulbs up here—just in case someone forgets to turn off the electricity. "Mother asked me to find out—"

"I . . . I . . . I'm all right. Just a . . . a headache."

Dad is tall, broad, craggy-featured—but gentle. He is not handsome, but he is not homely. He is reliable.

He leaned over and put his hand on my forehead. "You seem hot." I knew he was thinking about medicine for me. "Maybe the flu."

I wanted to be alone. "I'm just tired. I'll go to bed soon," I said, turning my head from him.

After he left, the light bothered me but I couldn't bring myself to leave the rocking chair long enough to turn it off. I just sat and stared. My eyes took in details in this large attic room which I'd missed before. I saw that one strip of wallpaper behind the old radio had been pasted on upside down. Two cobwebs decorated the far corner of the ceiling. How long had that ugly crack along the side of the long mirror been there?

After a time I dragged myself down to my bedroom. I didn't bother to wind my clock or to reset the alarm. As fast as I could, I got into my pajamas. But in bed I couldn't sleep. I lay in a ball, and waves and waves of fear pounded at me like surf. *Why had I run?* Now when they came for me, they'd punish me both for the accident and for running away.

I thought I did not sleep but I must have because I could smell coffee, and the morning sounds of showers and hurried feet scuffling down the hallways came to me. I lay there. The traffic on Mountain Pass increased and I realized from the speed of the cars that the fog must have disappeared.

Doors banged downstairs. The house quieted.

I felt a hand on my cheek. "Marilla, can I bring you something?" Mother went to the window and opened the shades a bit. My eyes followed her painfully as if there was grit under each lid.

My voice was scarcely audible. "I didn't sleep. I'm going to stay in bed."

"Good. That's what you need." She straightened my blanket and tucked it in around my chin. "I'll phone the school that you'll be absent."

Where was the truck now? Were the police examining the right front fender at this very minute?

I shut my eyes tightly. "And please phone Mrs. Osmund," I said.

I half dozed the day away. Every time the telephone rang I was frightened. Every car that came near our house sounded like a police siren.

Late in the afternoon I pulled on my robe and went down to sit in the living room where I could see when the paper boy threw the *Ledger* on our front porch. I waited. Always now, I would be waiting.

Finally, there he was.

Fortunately, Mother was talking on the telephone in the kitchen and nobody else was home, so I could have the newspaper to myself. But when I carried it back into the living room I couldn't immediately force myself to begin searching for the account of an accident last night. I had persuaded myself that the boy, whoever he was, was going to be all right. I couldn't bear now to discover that my wishful thinking was only that.

My fingers stuck to the newspaper. How strange! Where was the story?

There. On the front page of the second section: HIT-RUN VICTIM, 12, INJURED IN FOG. He was a newsboy and his name was Lyle Abbot. He was late delivering, delayed by the weather. He was badly hurt, much of the time in a coma. He had no father. The bicycle that he had earned himself, according to his mother, Mrs. Hannah Abbot, was completely wrecked. Whenever rational, he seemed to be fretting about it. At the moment he could not be questioned about the accident. But an attendant, Mrs. Gary Jones, said that he had been brought to the emergency door by a young man who probably had hit him.

"Young *man*," I gasped, dumbfounded.

Dropping the paper, I thought back. My blue jeans? My rumpled shirt and sweater? My clipped hair? My height? My carrying the boy? My hoarse, frightened voice. Really, as I recalled now, this Mrs. Gary Jones, busy as she was, never once had taken a solid look at me. Yes, she *could* have mistaken me for a boy.

I laughed crazily. "They're searching for a young m-man."

Then I began to cry.

Chapter

:7:

Because Dad always has so many late hours of work in the drugstore, Mother takes one course a semester at the Longwood Opportunity School. Right now she's on a painting kick. The night after the accident when Dad left for the store and Mother—after offering to stay home with me—departed for her Rosemaling class, I took the newspaper, paste, and a few of the plain postcards from the desk in the den, and retreated upward.

A long time I sat in the rocker, looking with dull eyes at the stuff I'd deposited on the old dining table, planning exactly what I'd do. I had thought I would go back to the hospital today, but I decided it was too risky. In mystery stories and on television the guilty party always returns to the scene of the crime—but I wouldn't. I'd stay away from the Mountain Pass dead end. I'd never go near the hospital.

My hair? No more hacking at it. Thank heavens, it grew like weeds. Should I start wearing skirts at Osmund's? But that might arouse curiosity.

How much did a new bicycle cost?

Well, I'd better get busy.

Carefully I cut out of the newspaper the printed names: *Lyle Abbot* and *Longwood Hospital*. These I pasted neatly on the address side of a postcard. Then I searched the newspaper for individual words. I found an *I* and an *am* but I had to use various-sized letters for *sorry*.

Now I put the scissors back in the sewing machine, packed away the postcards, paste, and newspaper in the second drawer in the desk in the cupola. There—absolutely safe! All day I'd been planning how to write to him without taking a chance on someone recognizing my handwriting.

Next day I returned to school, and afterward to the flower shop. I managed to give the right front of the old truck a once-over. As far as I could make out, it was battered about the same as usual. I knew, of course, that experts might find scratches and evidence that I couldn't see. Also, the chrome rim around the light bulged out, but I'd pound that back somehow.

On my way home I dropped the card in the big box outside the post office. My plan was to use a different mailbox each time.

That night I searched the *Ledger* from the beginning of the first column to the end of the last one. There wasn't a mention of the accident.

At first I felt relief, but it soon gave way to anxiety. If I couldn't learn about Lyle Abbot's condition through the newspaper, how would I find out? How would I know if he were improving or how long he had to stay in the hospital? As long as they thought it was a boy who had caused the accident, I couldn't telephone.

Again I took the scissors and paste and a postcard. The only full word that I could find in the paper tonight was *Longwood,* so the address I pasted on the postcard, made up of individual letters, was not as neat as last night's.

I decided I'd better say something about the bike if, as had been reported, that seemed to fret the injured boy. These words also were hard to put together. I ended with a rather crookedly pasted together *will PAY for biKE.*

The next noon I put this card in the mailbox near Kennedy High, not knowing when I mailed it what a feature I was building for the newspapers. Never had it occurred to me that a reporter could concoct a front-page article out of my first simple postcard saying that I was sorry. But there it was that night, hitting me right in the face and in the pit of my stomach when I picked up the *Ledger.*

You couldn't miss it. The story was near the bottom of the page, but it had been spaced across three columns so that a large headline could run across the top of it.

Again I got a shock.

I learned the police weren't hunting for an old panel truck which I had thought they'd find in a hurry. No. This Mrs. Gary Jones really couldn't describe the vehicle which brought the injured boy to the hospital. In the fog, and in the emergency, she'd only seen the front end of an old dark car. Sedan? Maybe. Dark—maybe black, maybe blue.

Why, I was practically secure. A young man in an old sedan!

Funny. I should laugh.

I wanted to die.

Now I knew that it was no simple accident that I had caused. I knew that Lyle Abbot had a brain concussion and a fractured skull, plus serious bruises. Much of the time he remained unconscious.

I sent another postcard.

I don't know about the injured boy, but certainly the *Ledger* welcomed these notes. They got people to comment on them. They quoted the boy's mother. "Sometimes his eyes are open and I think he hears and sees but I don't know how much," she said, and she told about reading my card to the boy. It seemed as if he understood. When she read my next card to him about paying for his bike, it seemed to her that he tried to respond.

That next Sunday I went through the drawers of my old desk, gathering together all the cash I'd earned. Dad says that with money I'm like a squirrel with nuts. I stash it away, safely, but only heaven knows where. I'm never quite sure how much I've saved from the flower shop, and the various jobs before that: baby-sitting, gardening, walking Mrs. Mellowes' dogs, etc. About twice a year, I decide to get financially organized, then I delve into all the nooks in the old desk, look in old jars and under cushions of the furniture in the attic—and generally, I quite surprise myself with my wealth. Lately Mother and Dad have been getting more insistent that I open a savings account since my flower shop money accumulates more regularly and quickly than money from my previous jobs—at least until that April Sunday in the attic.

That day I harvested all the money I'd hoarded. It made a nice pile.

I took a large, perfectly plain envelope from the desk in the den and sealed the bills in it. Now that the *Ledger* was devoting so much space to the newsboy's accident it was easy to find his printed name for the address. The envelope was heavy. I put two stamps on it.

In one way it gave me some relief to drop that fat envelope in the mail slot at the closed post office. In another way, I hurt. I had been hoping to use that money toward college.

Chapter
:8:

All this I relived after delivering the last May Day order to the newsboy in the hospital, and you may be sure that I was not in the mood for much golf. But if Seth was still waiting for me at Lloyd's I intended to get there.

It was dark.

I like the dark. I've always liked it. As I ran along Mountain Pass from our house to the big putting green alongside Lloyd's shack, I stopped occasionally to close my eyes and let the May breeze touch me lightly with fresh fragrance from the pines on the slopes.

Suddenly nostalgia hit me. How I wished I were *innocent* again! Spring had passed me by this year. I'd lost my seventeenth April. Usually I know which of the pools are free of ice each spring. I know where willows glisten with new vigor; where squirrels with a sweet tooth tongue the trickle of sap on the maples. I know where to find soft catkin tufts on the trembling aspens, and where the first skunk cabbage sends up its purple hoods.

"Well, it's about time!"

I snapped out of my reverie and saw Seth's tall frame lounging against the wire fence near the gate to the golf range. Even when he's no more than a silhouette in the dark I can tell whether or not it's Seth. Now when I heard the impatience in his voice it irked me. I was tired of rushing. I was tired of pressing. I was tired.

"Don't boss me! I've had enough of that at Osmund's."

"Why so late?"

"It's May Day, remember?" I added tartly, "Lots of abnormal kids are going to a high school dance tonight. They want corsages. You and I know that the normal thing to do is to practice, practice—"

"Rilla, what's eating you?"

"I don't know." I did know, but to divert him I told him something he could easily accept. "Eukie's been giving me a time. She's going to the dance tonight. She went through my things and—well, you can imagine how I reacted."

He nodded. He knows me, and he understands about Eukie.

Lloyd's Golf Range was flooded with light and in every practice stall someone was swinging away at a bucket of balls. Out over the field you could see white pellets flying in all directions above the round faces of the distance markers. You could hear the groaning "Oh, *no,*" from the duffers as they sliced, hooked, and whiffed. The putting green was overrun. Was every other person in the world playing golf these days?

We took our clubs and a large bucket of balls to the extreme west boundary of the field where there is some turf. Most golfers won't practice their short game. They want to stand on the rubber mat and try to hit the ball farther than across Texas.

Lloyd just shakes his head. "They don't know what separates the men from the boys. You can't tell them that good approach shots—from the fringe of the green to about one hundred yards out—that's the part of the game that decides the contests."

Seth dumped a pile of balls from the bucket.

"I'll shoot five, then you shoot five," he said. aim for that 100-yard marker." He selected a short iron from his bag and checked his grip on it. "We'll stick with the wedge up through the 8-iron tonight. That's all."

Why was Seth so grim? Granted, we are always serious about our game, but right then I longed for something in the nature of a light touch.

Why couldn't we be like the other couples out here? Why couldn't we be having fun?

Seth took some practice swings. I saw him hit a firm, crisp shot which started out directly for the marker. Then I took over. But I didn't do well. My mind was wandering.

This is bad. You can't have a wandering mind and play winning golf.

People who don't play the game can't realize

the mental discipline that is involved. Oh, you should hear Lloyd lecture on that: "Golf is 30 per cent physical and 70 per cent mental. Lose control of the mental side and you are only 30 per cent a golfer. To win—you have to be mentally tough."

Seth kicked a ball onto some turf. "I'm not swinging. I'm punching." Frowning, he waggled his club to loosen his wrists and then he hit what was about a 95 per cent perfect shot. Suddenly he spun on his heels and said, "Rilla, I'm worried about you."

"About *me?*" My club hit the ground with a thud. "Well, just let me worry about my own game. You take care of yours and I'll take care of mine."

His brows drew together over his eyes. "I feel responsible about you on the team."

"I *won* my position in the qualifying matches."

"I know, but I promoted you to the coach. I kept telling Mr. Moss there was nothing in our interscholastic rules yet saying a girl couldn't play on the high school golf team. I guess when they wrote the rules it just never occurred to anybody that a girl would play well enough to squeeze out the boys. So I feel responsible—"

"Well, thank you, Mr. Cone," I interrupted.

He was really scolding me now. "You should have been here earlier tonight, Rilla. This is no time to goof off. I've been here going on two hours."

"Well, just because you've got a rich father and don't have to work—" I don't know why I said that. His father is not rich. Seth actually wishes he could have a job.

I saw his mouth tighten and his eyes narrow. I wished he'd tell me off, but he didn't. He just stared at me, and pretty soon I realized he wasn't even seeing me. "S-Seth?" I faltered. He wasn't listening.

Wanting to bring him back in a hurry to Lloyd's range, I said, "Do I shake hands with my opponent tomorrow before we start the game?"

Seth straightened. "Not unless he puts out his hand." In a voice caught between friendship and irritation, he added, "You do when you finish, win or lose."

I grinned. "You mean when I *win* I shake hands with him."

Now he was really seeing me. He shook his head sadly, like a parent over a cocky child who is sure to meet his comeuppance. "No matter what happens tomorrow, keep trying. You may think you're beaten but you never know when your opponent will lose his touch."

"I know, I know. You sound just like Lloyd." And rolling my *r*'s I began the speech I've heard and re-heard for three years, whenever a new student signs up for golf: "There is no other game in which the influence of fear is so great as in golf. A player sees a sand trap, or he gets a bad lie in the rough, and he completely loses his concentration and his coordination."

For a moment Seth looked at me as if he had

a few hot words on his tongue that it would give him relief to get rid of. But he kicked some balls into a pile. "Suppose you put on your glove, Miss Marston, and show me some of your shots."

"I can't find my glove and I haven't the cash for a new one," I grumbled. I took a couple of practice swings but I was tight. My shots faded. It was discouraging. But the worst of it was —I couldn't seem to care. Usually I want to wrap a club around a tree if it fails me.

A faint "Anchors Aweigh" gave me an excuse to more shots but they weren't anything to get excited about. "I guess I don't want to practice," I said finally. "I'll try not to let you down tomorrow."

Seth said, "The person you can't let down is Lloyd. Everybody knows you're his protégée. You've got to be a good advertisement for him."

I groaned mightily. "This is getting complicated. I started out with the simple ambition of playing for Kennedy High. Now I've turned into a—"

"What's this, what's this?" came a deep baritone complaint. "Stop whistling! Honestly!" I hit a couple over my shoulder. "Jitters?"

It was Lloyd.

I smothered a despairing sound. I hoped he hadn't heard me grousing. Nothing will ever make me hurt Lloyd if I can help it. This man has been so wonderful to me!

He is a tall, lean person with long, sloping shoulders. He looks like the great athlete he was in his younger days. Now he has a thick thatch of pure white hair on his head, and long wrinkles in his cheeks that make him look like a dignified Indian chief. He moves with the ease and lightness of one, too. His voice is gentle, and his patience unfailing, but he expects discipline.

"I think you ought to call it a day," Lloyd said now. "There's such a thing as too much practice and wearing away your edge. But Rilla, watch that left side of yours. It's blocking your swing." Lloyd always says my name as if the *R* tickles his tongue.

He waited while we put our clubs away and we walked slowly toward his office. Lloyd generally is a quiet man, but he quite surprised me tonight. He said, "I expect you to win your match tomorrow, Rilla."

Taking a key from his pocket he unlocked a soft drink canteen and gave me and Seth a Coke. Standing there, watching the way the bright lights caught in his white hair, I thought about my thirteenth summer. The neighbors on Mountain Pass were incensed because some stranger had bought the old pasture at the city limits and was putting a business, a golf range, on their nice quiet street. What to do? Petition? But he was just over the Longwood city limits. The people of Mountain Pass could only smolder; they couldn't touch him.

I remember the indignation when a strong wire fence went around the land where we children had run wild. The extra traffic. The noise of cars. The bright lights at night.

I remember the evening when, angry and hurt about something or other at home, I slammed out of the house, ran blindly down the street, then found myself kicking yellow golf balls that had been driven outside the range. I looked around. Out in the field, on an old tractor with a big screen scoop attached to the front of it, the man who owned this new range was gathering balls to refill his buckets. He waved to me and I waved back. While I had his eye, I threw several balls onto the field to let him know there were lots outside the fence, too.

Driving the tractor close to where I was standing, he shut off the noisy engine. He looked me over, appraising me in a way that was new to me. At home usually it's, "Rilla, your socks don't match" or, "Rilla, comb that mop of hair." This man looked at my height, at my wide shoulders.

"You a golfer, girl?" he asked.

I shook my head. I liked him already—the way he talked, his deep voice, and the way he looked. The dignity with which he treated me soothed my ruffled pride.

He thought a moment. "I'll make a bargain with you. Each evening you take one of my buckets out here and pick up the balls. Then I'll lend you clubs and you can hit all you want free."

It sounded intriguing. It would give me something to do these summer evenings.

Lloyd and I settled into an immediate friendship.

Golf seemed to attract people from far and near

and Lloyd was doing a booming business. He had an assistant in the office but if they were both busy I sometimes sold the buckets of balls, rented the clubs, or raked the practice sand trap. Oh, there were lots of chores.

Lloyd started giving me bits of instruction. He told me I had good golf hands.

One morning during my third summer with Lloyd, when I was fifteen, I was pinching off dead petunias in the flower boxes he likes to keep blooming all season when I heard him call to me. "Rilla, I'd like you to meet someone who likes golf as much as you do." And that's how I met Seth Cone, the tall, thin young man whose family had just moved into the house next door to us.

Now, as Seth and I started to leave, Lloyd said, "Rilla, after the game, win or lose, come to see me. I have something I want to talk to you about. It's too late to go into it now. Good luck, Seth! I hope Rilla makes you proud tomorrow."

"I'll certainly try to," I said, glancing at Seth standing there with a faraway smile on his face. "I'll try."

Chapter :9:

It rained last night. That meant the course would play easier, I figured this morning while taking a quick shower before breakfast. I could pitch to the flags and the ball would stick. Swathed in the big bath towel, I peeked out the window to study the trees. The leaves were practically motionless. If only it stayed windless, that would be another break.

We gathered at the high school and Mr. Moss drove the squad in his station wagon to the Lamplighters Country Club where we'd been given permission to hold our match. There were five on the team: Seth was the number one man and I was number five. When we stowed our bags in the back of the station wagon, I noticed that the hoods Eukie had knit for my wooden clubs, red with white stripes, not only were the brightest part of all the equipment but they were the lone spots of school color. That means good luck for me, I told myself with a bit of wishful planning.

If anything, I think that having a girl in the car

kept the others from getting tense. They could tease me. Actually, Seth was the only quiet person. He was sitting in back and I was up in front with Mr. Moss, and I'd hardly have known he was with us if occasionally I hadn't caught a faint whistle. Even Mr. Moss kidded me. I could scarcely believe my ears. Mr. Moss is a moderately tall man with gray eyes that are deep-set and penetrating. When he shakes hands with you, you know he really has a golf grip. His conversation is that of a person who knows what he has to say, says it, and that's it. The team thinks he's hard, but fair.

While parking the station wagon, he said, "Remember—you'll feel pressure. But never forget, that same pressure is hitting your opponent."

We saw a group about our age over on the practice tee. Division's squad was already loosening up. Mr. Moss went into the pro shop and when he had registered for us he brought out a couple of buckets of yellow balls. Leading us to the far side of the practice tee, he watched while we each took some of the balls and swung. He didn't say much to the boys and, of course, he has never given me much instruction because he knows of my closeness to Lloyd.

"Oh, oh," I heard from the other group, "who's going to play the girl?"

I wasn't as nervous as I'd thought I would be. Probably I was too absorbed remembering what Lloyd had told me last night about my left side.

"Okay, gang," Mr. Moss said. "Seth—on the tee."

I stood a little apart from the others, over by the ball-washer, watching. The Lamplighters' clubhouse is a modern glass-and-brick building that seems to crouch on the tip of the hill. The starter's tee is on a plateau below it, and as I stood there looking down the 435-yard first hole, the fairway appeared to narrow. Suddenly it seemed like a slim slit of grass edged with trees and rough and salted with sand traps.

I took a deep breath. I watched Seth balancing himself for his first drive, and I felt wobbly. Was his heart dancing like mine? Was his breath coming in fast, quick spurts? "Just let him get off the first tee in respectable fashion," I prayed. "Then let me do the same without making a fool of myself."

I had the shakes. But I remembered Mr. Moss's words: my opponent would be feeling pressure, too.

Seth hit a long ball, a slice. The player with him hit a long one, a hook. Then they were off, practically galloping to their balls.

The number two men—another slice, and a banana ball.

The number three pair—two duck hooks.

"Everybody's nervous," I told myself, turning away. "They're rushing at the top of the backswing." I'd hit easy, I planned. I wouldn't go for distance, just for the center of the fairway so I could keep the ball in play.

"Rilla." It was Mr. Moss. "Good luck."

I moved to the first tee. My playing partner was shorter than I was. A smiling, round-faced, very clean-looking boy, he had the uptilted dark eyes of a person who has Oriental blood. I wished I'd caught his name. Jim? Tim? And the last name? Something like Too. I was too embarrassed to ask him to repeat it.

His handicap was one point lower than mine so, although we were playing even without handicap, he had the honors. He groaned at his drive but I'd be happy to get the same one, I thought, as I teed up my ball. There was a strange trembling in my wrists. I stepped back from my ball a moment, looked down the fairway, and all the hazards on the course jumped at me. So I took a deep breath and just hit as squarely as I could. When I looked up, I could see the ball way out, soaring right down the middle.

"Nice shot," said my partner, and we were off.

We both reached the first green in 3 and we both took two putts for a 5. "You play well for a girl," he told me.

While we walked to the second tee one of the Division players yelled to him, calling him by name, but I still didn't get it. This was stupid. I couldn't go on calling him *you*.

I pushed out, "I'm afraid I didn't catch your name."

"It's very simple. Timothy Too. It's my nick-name that confuses—Timtoo." He grinned. "I didn't get your name either." So I explained about Rilla, short for Marilla.

After we'd played a few holes we were still even. I sort of enjoyed that game. I wasn't making too many mistakes. Neither was Timtoo. It settled into being a question of who sunk his putts to take a hole. We see-sawed back and forth, and neither of us ever was up more than one hole.

Yes, I almost enjoyed it until we were coming in on the last hole, and then in the distance I noticed the entire two teams waiting for us near the last green, watching our every shot. "Oh, no," I moaned.

Timtoo heard me. "I see them too," he said.

We approached our second shot. Because his drive was a few feet longer than mine, I had to shoot first. As luck would have it I found I had a tight lie. My 5 wood? No, I couldn't reach the green with it. I'd gamble with my 3 wood.

It was a mistake. "I only got a nickel's worth of that ball," I groaned.

Timtoo said politely, "Too bad." Then he hit a shot that looked as if it were going right on the green. There was one lone elm tree in the fairway, but his ball was passing through thin little twigs high up in the tree. Then it hit something solid We could hear the smack but we couldn't see where the ball dropped. As luck would have it, we found it nestled right between the trunk and a big root.

Timtoo studied that ball for what seemed like five minutes. Finally he poked it out backhand with his putter. There was nothing else he could do. He had to waste that shot.

And by that one piece of bad luck for him I won by a stroke.

"I hope I get a chance to play you again," I said, shaking hands.

I heard Mr. Moss call: "Hurry, Rilla, the photographer is waiting. We'll let him take his picture, then we'll post our scores."

I wondered—why a photographer for a high school match? Was this for our yearbook? The man with the camera who was in such a hurry lined the players from Kennedy in a row, me in the middle, each of us holding our driver down on the ground toward the camera. Seth was on one side of me and Rex Small, our mailman's son, on the other.

"I wish I had a comb," I whispered to Seth, brushing back my hair with my hand.

"You're letting it grow too long."

Instantly I changed the subject. "Is Division going to have a picture taken too?"

"I don't think so."

"Why not?"

"They don't have a girl on the golf squad." He added briefly, "And we won."

I gave him a troubled glance. "Who is the photographer?"

"He's from the *Ledger*."

A feeling of panic welled in me. My picture in the *newspaper?* Suppose the nurse at Longwood

Hospital should read the Sunday paper and see this photograph? Would she recognize me? I started to tremble.

"Will the young lady hold her head up a bit?" the photographer said.

I wanted to shout: "I won't have my picture taken!" Maybe I could move my head just as he snapped—make myself a blur?

"Stop trembling," said Seth. "You've finished today's business. Smile."

I forced a smile, aware only of a stupid desire to cry. Was this going to be my life from now on? Sudden alarms? I could almost picture it: afraid to go around corners, afraid to meet new people, afraid—always afraid.

Gone was my glad excitement over winning, vanished was my pride in not letting Kennedy High School down.

"Ready?" said the photographer.

Chapter

: 10 :

Curious because of Lloyd's parting words to me the night before, I hurried through my supper and ran through the pelting rain to the golf range, afraid that because of the weather I might find it closed. But Lloyd was there and he seemed to be glad to drop the paper work he was doing to talk to me. Under the lone hanging bulb his white hair was like a cap of snow.

"Tell me everything," he said when I burst in and shook the rain from me like a water spaniel.

Tell him everything? That's all the invitation a golfer needs. Shot by shot I replayed the day's game for him.

"I knew I was doing all right," I said, feeling rather subdued, "but I wish I hadn't beaten Seth's score. He tied for worst score on our team. I couldn't believe my ears. We wouldn't have won if Rex Small hadn't shot his all-time low." I broke off, shrugging, mystified.

Turning on his heel Lloyd walked to the window and stared out at the rain. His fingers tap-danced on the pane. "What has Seth told you about his parents?" Lloyd asked, over his shoulder.

I stared, dumbfounded. "His parents?"

"Has he mentioned trouble at home?"

Immediately my mind raced to, and settled on, the kind of trouble we have around our home. "Why, his dad makes plenty of money. When a man sells real estate he makes good commissions. Seth doesn't have to worry at all about getting through college—except lately, his grades."

In a voice that was so muffled I could hardly distinguish his words, Lloyd said, "I don't mean money trouble. I only wish it were something simple like that."

I stood, motionless. You could even hear my breathing. The shocked silence held.

I was embarrassed. Maybe Lloyd was too, and maybe he wished he hadn't started this conversation, because he changed it abruptly. "I have a nice surprise for you, Rilla. The Jones-Galen Manufacturing Company bought the Madison Heights golf course for their employees. They want to enter the golf meets this season. The district, and the state, and it would be good advertising for Jones-Galen to have winners on their team."

"Oh?"

"Their personnel director got in touch with me. Asked me about golfers who practice here. How'd you like to try for a summer replacement job at Jones-Galen? If you get it you'd play golf on that nice course."

My hands went to my cheeks. "Oh, Lloyd." Surely this was too wonderful to be true! In a breathless voice I said, "A course like *that!* And a chance at a job so I can work and play there this summer!"

Lloyd shook his head. "They wouldn't be doing you such a favor. Girl, you don't seem to know it, but you're a pretty darned good golfer!" He scratched his head. "When's your birthday? When'll you be eighteen?"

"The week I graduate."

"Good." He nodded. "Real good."

I wanted to dance. I wanted to laugh. I thought I might cry. I said hurriedly, "This is too wonderful to be true. I need money—oh, how I need it! And there isn't enough to do at Mrs. Osmund's for me to work full time this summer. I was thinking I might have to go in my dad's drugstore and I don't want that." I cleared my throat. "You sure are a good friend to me, Lloyd," I said.

A sudden thought came to mind: "Are you . . . will you recommend . . ." I paused, then added, "anybody else?"

Lloyd shook his head slightly. "Seth can't take a summer job. He's going to college as soon as he graduates from Kennedy." I looked surprised. He tipped his head curiously. "Hasn't he told you that?"

I could feel my mouth drop open. "Seth—going to summer school?"

"Not summer school. Tech Institute is on the quarters system. He's starting right away in the summer quarter." He commented flatly, "Wants to get away from Longwood, I guess."

"I . . . I don't believe that."

But I did! Like that, my joy over my own summer vanished.

I made up an excuse about having to get home in a hurry, and after I'd said good-bye to Lloyd and shut his door against the rain I started for Mountain Pass. However, I knew I wasn't ready to go home.

I passed our house, lighted up as if electricity were free. Then I passed Seth's house with one dim light in the living room window—the burglar light. If I were planning to break into a house I'd consider such a light an invitation. I'd know nobody was there.

Hunching my shoulders against the drizzle, I continued walking. If you'd asked me, I suppose I would have said I was walking aimlessly. Unconsciously I must have been looking for comfort because when I realized how far I had hiked I saw I was within a block of Dad's drugstore. I was tired. I'd wait for closing time and drive home with him.

Dad seemed to be nowhere around but the clerk said he was in the little back alcove where he makes up prescriptions. I had phoned him after the game to tell him the good news. Now his eyes lit up when he saw me. "Congratulations, Rilla. Come here to celebrate?"

"Just took a long walk, Dad. Thought I'd ride home with you."

Nodding, he continued counting pills into a bottle.

Sitting on his high stool, I watched the store in the big, curved detection mirror that hangs on a post right in line with Dad's lookout from the back room. The concave mirror is positioned high above the counters; from where I was sitting I could see up and down every aisle in the drugstore. Some respectable people in the neighborhood would be quite astonished to learn what Dad knows about them and pilfering. Shoplifting has been the subject during many meals at home. Dad won't let a youngster get away with a thing; he doesn't want to be morally responsible for any bad habits starting because he has kept silent. But each older person is a separate problem. And if they only do it once, he usually lets it go by.

"I'm hungry," I said impulsively, witnessing in the mirror a huge sundae that passed across the counter.

Dad sighed. "There go the profits."

"How much longer?"

"About fifteen minutes."

While the clerk fixed me a chocolate and strawberry ice cream cone, I went to the magazine rack to find something to read during the next fifteen minutes. An issue of a national picture magazine struck my eye. Even though I had seen it before, my eyes seemed to burn as I read: LONGWOOD'S HIT-AND-RUN TRAGEDY.

I took the magazine and scurried back to the alcove. "Don't spill on it," Dad muttered without looking at me, his habitual warning when I borrow one of his magazines.

I'd lost my appetite. I wished I could throw away my ice cream but that would look peculiar.

My finger ran down the index column. *The Haunted Boy.* I searched for page 76.

That young man was supposed to be me. I stared at the picture of him sitting in the long hospital corridor.

I moaned.

If only I hadn't run!

I was brought back to the drugstore by Dad's sharp scolding. "I told you, Rilla, don't spill on the merchandise."

With my handkerchief I tried to make a neat job of wiping melted ice cream from the face of the young man who was supposed to be me. "I . . . I am sorry, Dad," I said. "I was reading about the hit-and-run."

"Pathetic case," he said mechanically, still counting.

"Pathetic?"

"Obviously the young man isn't cut out to be a criminal. Too bad he has to spend his life hiding."

"Maybe that's just the story the newspapers give about him."

"No. Look at the money he sends to the hospital."

I thought of my raided bank account which I hoped I'd be able to fatten up if I got the Jones-Galen job.

"Do you think it's enough? That is, will it pay for everything?"

"Oh, no, not nearly."

I sat up straight. "Why not? Good heavens, how much does a hospital cost?" I became indignant and my voice rose shrilly. "What do poor people do when they get sick? Are they just supposed to die on the street because hospitals are so expensive?"

My father glanced over his shoulder at me. I realized my voice had become almost hysterical but, after all, this was the very first time I had ever, in any way, discussed the hit-and-run case with anybody. I had made up my mind I wasn't going to give myself away; not by my handwriting, not by my voice, and surely not because my hair had been cut like a boy's. Now I had almost done it.

Scared by the way Dad was looking at me, I said heartily, "Well, the boy will probably be out of the hospital pretty soon and back to school."

"I doubt it."

"Why?"

Dad murmured one of those long Latin names that roll off his tongue so easily. It sounded awesome.

"What does that mean?"

"Blood clot on the brain. Tricky business." He shook his head.

I gulped. "Will he have to stay in the hospital a long time?"

"Probably." Dad went to his typewriter. After writing instructions on labels, he pasted them on the bottles. "I certainly hope there's some kind of compensation to cover the case."

My throat dry and tight, I murmured, "I certainly hope so."

Brushing my hand over my damp hair, I looked sideways at my father as he wrapped brown bottles. "How do you happen to know what's wrong with the Abbot boy?"

Instantly I wished I hadn't mentioned that name. How easy it is to make a slip! I bit my lower lip.

My father seemed unaware of my blunder. "Read about it in last night's *Ledger.*"

Oh? I pushed up my sleeves. Come to think of it, after my scene with Eukie over the beads and then fleeing to the third floor minus the *Ledger,* I had not even seen last night's issue.

Was May Day just twenty-four hours ago?

My father turned on the night light over the safe. "I just hope," he said, "that the newsboy doesn't die."

Chapter
: 11 :

I must have cried while I slept because when I awakened this morning my pillow was damp. *I just hope that the newsboy doesn't die.* My mirror told me I never had been so unattractive. Heavy eyes. My skin pale under my tan. And my hair—I hated my hair at this in-between length. I didn't know what to do with it. Oh, for the good old days when I could pounce on a straying lock with my manicure scissors; I always felt neat and trim and never in need of a comb.

At the breakfast table Jimbo was gobbling the Sunday funnies with his bacon and eggs. Jeffrey had to stay in bed because he had a sore throat. Eukie was yawning and sipping her latest diet concoction and looking at the newspaper. "How is our celebrity this morning?" She was looking at the picture on the sports page.

Suddenly I remembered the photographer from the *Ledger*. I'd been so disturbed by all that had happened since he had posed the golf team that I had actually forgotten to dread the result of that posing. I half rose from my chair. "May I have the paper?"

Eukie said, "I'm not through with it. You wait your turn."

Jumping from my chair I ran behind her and attempted to examine the newspaper over her shoulder, but she shifted, hunching over the sheet. "Eukie, please," I pleaded. "I've got to see the picture. What do I look like? Can you tell if it's me?"

"Well, well. What do you look like? Can I tell it's you? Will everybody know it's Miss Marilla Marston? My, my!" With a teasing smile she peeked under the printed page which she kept folded from my eyes. "I'll say this, the picture flatters you. Does that make you happy?"

I swallowed, and my hand moved to my throat. Finally Eukie gave me the paper.

I scanned the *Ledger*. Eukie must have been having fun with me. There was no picture of a group of young golfers holding their drivers on the ground toward the camera. The only golfing shot was of two people on a green, putting, one head down, leaning over the ball, and the other in the background—why, that was Timtoo!

I stared at the head turned to line up the direction of the putt. Me! But even I hadn't recognized myself. "Thank heavens," I sighed under my breath. Without telling us, the *Ledger* man had snapped a shot of my opponent and me when we reached the last green. I guess the group picture hadn't turned out. Maybe I'd been successful in my scheme when I jerked my head.

Taking a deep, luxurious breath, I managed to retrieve a little composure. For a time, once again, I was safe. For a time, once again, I was anonymous. "Kennedy High School's secret weapon." That's what the caption said about me.

"What?" I gasped, conscious of Jimbo punching my arm.

"You're taking me to the zoo. Before Mama went to church she said you would." He pushed his hand across his mouth, brushing toast crumbs into his lap and onto the floor. "We gotta get started. We want to get there before it's crowded so I can see things for our themes."

"Themes?"

"Yes. The whole class—we've been assigned to write about 'My Day at the Zoo.' "

I laid my knife and fork precisely across my plate. "I suppose it never occurred to anyone that I might have plans of my own. After all, I don't have too many free hours."

Eukie gave me a cool scrutiny. "I'm supposed to start dinner and take care of Jeffrey, and you're to take Jimbo to the zoo."

Under the cover of the table my hands clung to each other. I bit my lower lip. And at this highly inconvenient moment for me, when I would have liked to let go and weep to relieve some of the tight ache inside me, at this moment Eukie said, "We'll all have to be careful with Rilla."

"Why?" Jimbo wanted to know.

"Well, Seth's leaving sooner than she expected. Maybe her heart's breaking."

I stiffened.

First Lloyd. Now Eukie. I was hearing about Seth's leaving home shortly after Kennedy's graduation exercises from everybody but Seth. Why hadn't he told me?

Part of me despised myself for my suspicion but another part of me was suddenly intensely jealous of Eukie. I stared at her moodily, my fingers clutching the edge of the table. While I'd been working for Mrs. Osmund and had been engrossed in a terrible personal trouble, had she been building up a friendship with Seth?

I watched Eukie's graceful, small-boned hands play with her coffee cup. I couldn't bring myself to look at her face. I knew her clear blue eyes with their wide-open stare would be fixed on me and I had the feeling that I wanted to hide.

Jealous, I'm jealous, I thought with dismay.

I took my handkerchief and wiped it across my eyes. I was remembering that Eukie is two years older than I am, but there are only a few months' difference in her age and Seth's.

I was recalling that her lighthearted chatter had, through the years, won her the attention of almost any young man who'd momentarily caught her fancy.

Maybe Seth found he could relax with her. Maybe in the face of difficulties, golf was not so important to him. Maybe that was why he had played so poorly yesterday; he just didn't care. Couldn't concentrate. Could be, yes, it could be that my intense determination to make the squad only irritated him.

He'd helped me practice, sure, but that might have been a carry-over.

Suddenly I became aware that my head was swimming and I felt hot.

"Why, Rilla!" Eukie spoke, her voice sounding far away. "You know, I don't think I've ever seen you cry before."

Chapter
: 12 :

I was still upset and wanted to take it out on Jimbo as I slammed out of the house and reluctantly slid behind the wheel of our old car.

Often I've helped the kids with homework. I've griped, but I've helped them. Today was a call above duty. It wasn't fair of their teacher to give them an assignment that forced someone else in each of the students' families to give up time needed for other things in order to go to the zoo.

Resentfully, I backed our car out the narrow driveway and didn't realize Seth was watching from the Cones' breezeway. It was Jimbo who spotted him. And it was Jimbo who yelled: "C'mon along, Seth. We're going to the zoo." It was Jimbo who insisted, "C'mon. It'll be fun."

In my depressed state of mind nothing would have made me invite Seth to join us. Much as I wanted him to come along I was too self-conscious by now to be casual with him. Thank heavens for Jimbo!

Seth looked at me.

"If you'd like . . ." I began diffidently.

"Your car is too close to the lamppost," he answered obliquely.

"I wish you'd drive."

"Slide over."

Just like that, I was wearing a pair of rose-colored glasses. Just because I was sitting beside Seth I was filled with love and gratitude toward Eukie, Jimbo; all of a sudden the world was pretty much all right. Seth drove along the outskirts of town and, to avoid traffic, he took Shoefactory Road, which I never would have dreamed of doing because it crosses two state highways where there aren't lights to give you your turn through the heavy traffic.

Crossing Highway 90 wasn't bad. But when we came to Highway 86 we got caught in such a long line of autos that it took nearly ten minutes to cover the last block to the *Stop* sign.

Waiting in the sun there, the car began to feel like a furnace. Ordinarily there would have been plenty to talk about with Seth, but today when I began a subject I felt so nervous about saying the wrong thing that I actually was tongue-tied. Golf? No, not after his poor game in the match, and after mine was better than his. Let him bring up that subject first. School? That was ticklish too. He would have to tell me about that himself.

"Cut it out." I punched at Jimbo who had just banged the back of my head.

He leaned over the back of the seat and, scrounging his head down, tried to see out the front window between Seth and me. "We've been here all day. There ought to be a cop at a corner like this."

"There is." Seth had the window open on his side. He leaned way out. "I can see a red light flashing."

"Something's happened." Jimbo tried to open the door on my side. "I want to go see."

"You stay here." Seth turned on the ignition again. "We're about to move."

We did move. Slowly. And when we finally reached the corner we saw that something really had happened: a nasty accident with two cars bashed in, glass all over the road, and a sports car standing at a crazy angle on the road's shoulder. There was a police car and an ambulance.

I stared at a young man standing forlornly by one of the wrecked cars, his shoulders hunched over, his hands jammed into the pockets of his tight cotton slacks, his foot kicking the tire. On his face was a blending of emotions—despair, rage, frustration. If he were one of the drivers in the accident, at least he didn't run away. Better to face the misery now, I thought, than to be haunted forever after.

"You're making such funny noises, Rilla." Seth was watching me with frank curiosity. "You scared?"

"Oh, I . . ." I shivered. "I guess I just don't like to see people get hurt." I gazed at the young man kicking at the tire. "Do you suppose he was one of the drivers?"

"If it was his fault he'll lose his driver's license," Seth said, speeding across the intersection as the policeman directed. "He looks as if he's under eighteen."

I asked in dismay, "Does that make a difference?"

"You should know it does," he said impatiently. "You had to study the state's manual for motorists. You couldn't get your license without practically memorizing the guide for safe driving. If you don't comply with the safety laws your license is suspended, sometimes revoked."

Now an entire avenue of new, depressing thoughts had opened for me. Not until this moment had it occurred to me that every time I drove a car since April Fools' Day I might be committing a new crime. Now I'd *have* to give up my job delivering for Mrs. Osmund, even if I wasn't lucky enough to get the Jones-Galen work this summer.

"Park here on the street," said our businessman, Jimbo, interrupting my thoughts. "We don't want to pay fifty cents to use the zoo's parking lot. We can walk from here."

All of Longwood county seemed to be there ahead of us. "I wonder if *every* teacher thought up 'My Day at the Zoo,' " I grumbled.

We managed to stay together while we toured the aviary. Birds aren't as popular as monkeys or we would have lost each other in the crush. We tried to pronounce bird names—*whydahs* and *chloropsis* and *touraco* and such. Jimbo pulled a small notebook from his pocket but he didn't have a pencil. He borrowed one from Seth.

Seth told him, "Let's meet in one spot in one hour in case we lose each other."

We settled on the refreshment stand, which is visible from almost every part of the zoo.

Then Jimbo was gone. Seth and I were alone.

"What's your pleasure?" he asked. "Want some peanuts for the elephants?"

"I want peanuts for Rilla."

Ambling along slowly, we aimed for whatever attraction seemed to draw the least crowd. It was hot. We tried to stay in the shade, but the shade was crowded too. Longwood Zoo is a modern park with the animals living in structures that look as if they were blueprinted by a mad architect, but the animals—if they could talk—would say they liked the craziness better than barred cages.

Despite all the openness the smells in a zoo are not the most fragrant. Long before the hour was up Seth and I retreated to a little hill back of the refreshment stand, and now the frying of hamburgers and onions wasn't to our liking so we backed farther up the slope, away from the trees.

Seth lay on the grass. I sat beside him curling dandelion stems.

"What's on your mind, Rilla?"

"Nothing."

"Still thinking about that accident?"

I started. "How did you know?"

"It sure jarred you."

"It sure did."

"You've always been a strange girl." He smiled gently. "You pick up a snake without a thought, yet you get sick at the sight of blood."

Out of the corner of my eye I looked at the long flat length of him, prone on the grass, his healthy sunburn contrasting with the clean white of his sport shirt. He stared straight up into the sky, his brows drawn together, his eyes half-closed.

I moistened my lips with the tip of my tongue. Let's see, it was now five weeks. I was conscious of time lately: hideously conscious of the passing days. They ought to be putting a padding between April Fools' Day and me. Why, I wondered bleakly, didn't I begin to feel safer? Wasn't I ever going to be rid of this anxiety? What would I be doing by this time tomorrow? A month from now—where would I be?

Had I groaned?

Startled, I turned to look at Seth, to discover him wearing a rather shamefaced expression. The groan had come from him and he was annoyed with himself.

I thought ruefully, we're both hiding secrets from each other.

To cover his embarrassment, Seth spoke impulsively, "Are you taking the Jones-Galen job for the summer?"

"Lloyd mentioned something to me. Sounds good. I think I'll try for it. Mrs. Osmund certainly has been nice to me but I need more money."

"Don't we all!" Rolling over on his side, he propped his head in his hand. With the forefinger of his free hand he blocked the pathway of an ant intent on its own business. There was an almost fierce expression on his face as he teased the innocent ant, and suddenly I could not bear this splintering of the bond between Seth and me.

I said bluntly, "You ought to try for a Jones-Galen job. If they want a good golfer to represent them, you're it."

"I can't."

"That's what Lloyd said."

I fidgeted, pinching a dandelion leaf into tiny tucks. "And Eukie! You seem to be telling your plans to everybody except me."

He drummed on the ground, deep in thought. When he lifted his face, there was a despair in his eyes I had never seen before. "If I tell other people I'm starting college right away, that's it. But I knew if I started talking to you, Rilla . . ."

He paused, and I could hear him draw a heavy breath. "I knew I'd go into an explanation that I didn't want to about things at home!"

I dusted the dandelion bits from my lap. I didn't know what to say.

Seth's voice shaded to a deeper timbre. "At first I thought I'd drag out my school days, even flunk in high school. I was glad I had lost credits when we moved to Longwood and I had to take an extra year in high school—as glad as I was mad when it happened. As long as I could, I'd be a responsibility that would keep my parents together. Maybe they'd work something out."

I gasped.

He shook his head. "But now, I've given up. I'm going to get through college in three years if I can and get out of their way so they can do what they want."

It was funny to think that I've been living right next door to Mr. and Mrs. Cone for three years, never once dreaming there was trouble of any kind.

Through my mind mulled all the things I could recall about Seth's parents. I've been in and out of their house frequently, but when you come right down to it, I don't really know either his mother or his father very well.

For one thing his father seldom is home at the time I am likely to be there. Selling real estate the way he does, he has to make himself available to customers at hours that are convenient for them—Sundays, holidays, nights too. He works a lot at night. Mr. Cone is a tall, long-legged man—quick, restless, assertive—with an easygoing, boyish charm, and a punchy, slangy manner of talking.

Mrs. Cone is a tiny, doll-like woman, a real charmer—except that she wears too much makeup.

Her house is fussy, for my taste. I don't see how two big men like Seth and his father can live in it. It has scads of velvet pillows, and a crystal cat that climbs up the drapes. It has satin bows around the sheets and towels in the linen closet, which was open when I was there one day, and once I saw Mrs. Cone's dressing table—what a maze of creams and powders!

No wonder Seth is more comfortable in our house.

But it isn't the interior decoration in the Cone home as compared to ours that makes him at ease with us. He hasn't ever said so but he loathes being an only child. He can't stand the concentration of interest that is showered on him because there's no one else to share it.

I stared at him as he lay there, moodily chewing bits of clover. His face was tense, his eyes guarded.

"My mother's accusing my father of things that . . ." His fingers tightened on a stick and it snapped. "He *has* to work evenings. He *has* to work weekends. If he's going to sell houses he *has* to drive other women around. Oh, I don't know what's gotten into my mother. She wasn't like this before we moved to Longwood."

"Maybe something happened?"

"Maybe." Seth bit off the word as if it tasted bad on his tongue.

My, how hot it was. Tanned as I am, I could feel my arms toasting in the sun. A haze danced in front of my eyes. I wished I'd brought dark glasses.

Seth cleared his throat. Half closing his eyes, he began talking, dredging up his first summer on

Mountain Pass. Did I remember? The hard time he'd had getting to use the family car that summer? "Remember the night of your birthday, June the fifth?" His parents had gone off with another couple and he was left to polish the chrome on the car. The instructions: put it in the garage when he was through. Absolutely no driving!

I nibbled at one of my nails. "But we did drive some place, didn't we?"

"Just around the block a few times. I was showing off," he confessed. "I didn't want you to think my parents made a baby of me."

I frowned. "What about that particular night? Anything special?"

"Do you remember losing one of your birthday presents?"

"I can't remember . . . oh, yes. That makeup kit Eukie gave me."

"You lost it under the front seat of our car."

"Is *that* where it went?" How angry Eukie had been! Losing her gift even before I'd used it—or before she'd had a chance to borrow it from me. But what a silly present to give *me*—why not golf balls?

I flicked an ant from my ankle. "Why didn't you return it?"

"I didn't find it," he said jerkily. "My mother did." After a pause he added in a strained voice, "I think that's when things started going bad. If only I'd explained when I heard them quarreling about it; if only I'd said the bag under the front seat is

Rilla's. But if I had, I'd have had to tell how it got there, that I'd driven the car when I'd been forbidden to do so."

"But that would have been better than letting your mother think what she did think."

He gave me a sidelong glance. "That isn't the way it looked when I was sixteen. Remember that first time I drove you to the movies, and the traffic cop—"

"Oh, yes!" There had been a new *Stop* sign at the Victory Theater corner. We had come to a rolling pause, not a full stop, according to the officer who'd been parked in the shadow of the theater billboard. We had to go to the police station to hear a lecture about safe driving, then wait for Mr. Cone to come in a taxi to drive us home. When the policeman told him that Seth would lose his driver's privilege for thirty days, Mr. Cone shouted, "He's losing it for the whole summer!"

I nodded. Yes, I remembered.

"Car trouble, when you've just started to drive, is terrible trouble. So I went on letting my mother think it was some other woman's makeup kit." His face was dark and his voice was rough, not Seth's voice at all. "I went on hoping things would straighten out. And the longer I waited, the harder it got to confess."

"That's understandable," I said.

It isn't often you can completely understand another person's feelings as well as I could understand how Seth had felt. This business of being guilty—

Seth and I were both amateurs at it; neither of us knew how to cope.

But in the past few weeks I'd learned there was something about wrongdoing that splits you right down the middle—the desire to hide, the yearning to confess.

The load is unbearable. When you can't talk yourself free, sometimes you try to write yourself free—as I'm doing now, scribbling in an old notebook which will be hidden in my private desk in my private cupola.

Have you ever noticed what people keep diaries? Those people who get involved in horrid lawsuits. Women with scandals in their lives. Corrupt men. It makes a person wonder why they write down such junk as they do, but I suppose it's for the same reason as I have, to get out from under a burden.

Hard to confess, Seth said. I bit my lip so hard I thought it would bleed.

I had an almost uncontrollable longing to confess to Seth. Could it be the heat? Something unaccountable was happening to me. A nightmarish feeling of having lost my will power overwhelmed me. I couldn't stop myself.

Unable to control my tongue, I heard myself blurt, "You've confessed, and it wasn't so bad. I'll match you. I'll confess too."

I seemed mesmerized. "I'm the haunted boy the *Ledger* writes about."

Dead silence from Seth!

"I'm a hit-and-runner!"

I wished suddenly that I could lose consciousness. I was so close to a blackout, why couldn't I go all the way? With trembling fingers I jabbed my handkerchief at my eyes.

"Well?" I croaked. "How about that for a confession?"

I saw the line of Seth's throat and his head go rigid. Something happened to his mouth. An almost fierce expression came over his face.

He said curtly, "I don't think that's funny, Rilla."

He didn't believe me! I had another chance.

Like a swimmer out of breath, I gasped, "Guess it was a poor joke."

"I wouldn't have told you about the trouble at home if I'd thought . . . well, it's not a joking matter to me, Rilla."

"I'm sorry, Seth," I almost whimpered. "I . . . I shouldn't have said what I did."

Rolling over, he lay with his face cradled in his crossed arms. Minutes dragged past, slow, interminable.

About a year later, it seemed, Seth heaved himself into a sitting position. "I know you were only trying to make me feel better."

I turned to look at him. Sudden tears hung in my eyes.

The controlled smile left his face. "Rilla," he said softly. He leaned toward me. Gently, tenderly, he touched a soft finger to the outline of my mouth. "Don't cry about my family, Rilla," he said, half pleading and half laughing. "We Cones will fight it out somehow." He was watching me with open concern. "Rilla," he said, strangely solemn.

And then, before man and animal and *everybody,* he touched my lips with his, and I couldn't breathe . . . I simply couldn't breathe.

Chapter

: 13 :

Today, the forty-eighth day after the accident, it happened. I know it is the forty-eighth day because I have been *X*-ing out days on the Currier and Ives insurance calendar which hangs over the sewing machine in the attic.

Right after school I rushed off to the flower shop. Mrs. Osmund's round, full-moon face looked harassed. One of the Smithies hadn't shown up for work and Mrs. Osmund's feet were "crucifying" her again.

"At last, there you are," she greeted me as if I were hours late instead of dead on time. "Now you can make the posters. Are you any good at lettering?"

"What do you want on the posters?" I asked, not too surprised at this job or any other that Mrs. Osmund asked me to do.

She put a finger to her cheek. *"Watch for our Weekend Special."* Momentarily she pondered. *"Forty-nine cents* . . . put that in red ink, the rest in black."

"What is the weekend special?"

"Ah, I haven't decided. Maybe geraniums."

"We've got scads of begonias."

She pursed her tiny lips. "Make it *Specials.*"

Parking my books, I went down into the workshop in the basement. In the winter we always have to use the electricity down here, but today there was plenty of daylight coming through the small high windows above my head. With a yardstick I measured off word space on two white cardboard squares. This was a new job for me, so I ruined a couple of pieces of cardboard before I got what I wanted.

I was blocking in the letters with a heavy black crayon when I became conscious of a shadow moving across the window that opened onto the space where the delivery truck is kept, close to the back door.

I looked up. Nothing. But then I heard what sounded like a short-wave radio.

With a start, I thought, could it be *the police?*

Scared, I kept watching the window until I saw what I dreaded—the uniformed legs of an officer circling the old panel truck.

Crouching over the white cardboard on the big worktable, I could hear my own breathing, and my hand made such a tight fist around the crayon that my knuckles were white.

"Rilla!" I hadn't heard Mrs. Osmund come down, but in a vexed voice she said, "I distinctly told you *forty-nine cents.* Are you trying to bankrupt me? Thirty-nine, indeed."

"What's the policeman doing?" I whispered.

"What policeman?"

"Outside—by the truck."

She was still annoyed with me. "Run out and see."

I shook my head. "I can't. Haven't got time," I added quickly. "These signs—I'll have to start over." I mumbled, "Sorry about my mistake. Don't pay me for the time I've wasted."

"What's wrong with you today, Rilla?" Mrs. Osmund demanded in a baffled tone. "You're not yourself."

"What is myself?" I laughed shortly, flustered by this attention which I didn't want.

She shifted from one aching foot to the other. "Go see what the police want with your truck."

"My truck," I protested. I put down the black crayon—carefully. All right, I'd find out what the police wanted!

Rushing up the back steps I stumbled outside to where the panel truck was parked. "Hello," I muttered.

Before my eyes the uniform blurred and I blinked as I struggled to focus clearly.

"I want to speak to somebody about this truck," the officer said in an impersonal voice.

"I drive it—sometimes."

"Do you know when it was last tested for safety? We're having a checkup campaign "

I shook my head, my eyes sliding to the notebook he held in his hand. Safety campaign? I didn't believe him.

All he did, though, was give me some routine instructions, and when he finished, I nodded dumbly and groped my way back to the basement workshop.

Mrs. Osmund asked, "What did he want?"

"You have to take the truck over to the Wells Avenue station for a safety check. Monday afternoon." I swallowed hard.

My boss moaned. "I just can't afford a new truck yet." She threw up her hands. "Well, you take it over after classes on Monday."

"Me? *No!*" I cried. I had decided that I was never going to drive the truck again. I positively would not go near the police with it, even for a safety test. "No!" I cried again.

"It's your job to drive the truck," Mrs. Osmund said with unusual sharpness. "You know how busy I am."

"You ask me to do all kinds of things, and I do them," I said, my voice rising hysterically. "But I won't drive the truck again. I'm through—I'm quitting."

"Through?" Mrs. Osmund repeated. Well, she was sorry to see me go, but it might be wise to get a full-time assistant. And she started up the steps.

I stood there for a while without moving. Was I fired—or had I quit? I didn't know. The important thing was: here I am without work, without any more pay checks.

And I needed money. How I needed it! I had an obligation.

Chapter

: 14 :

Morning. Almost dawn. The day birds are rousing each other with querulous chirps. The eastern sky is tinged with gold, and the woods at the top of the high hill in back of our house are tipped with light, but down here on Mountain Pass it's still dark.

Dark—even up here in the attic where I prowl when I can't sleep.

I am quiet. I don't want to waken anyone.

Yesterday, on June fifth, I was eighteen.

This evening, in cap and gown, I'll be marching to the stage of the auditorium in Kennedy High School for my diploma. About three hundred of us will try to keep step to Mendelssohn's "Processional." We'll sing the school hymn. There'll be speeches, toasting the past, and the future, and then a solo by Anita Valencia. Our principal, Mr. Douglas, will present our class to the superintendent of public schools, T. G. Nichols, and, in turn, Mr. Nichols will present us with diplomas.

To speed up the program, Mr. Nichols will give

each of us the first diploma he lays his hands on, and tomorrow we're to visit the principal's office and exchange what we got for what we ought to get.

This afternoon at two o'clock (and I tremble thinking of it because it's so important to me) I have an interview scheduled at Jones-Galen.

I've got to get a job there! Any kind of work.

I've got to, got to . . .

I haven't been sleeping well lately. I don't know what a full night's rest is any more. Queer, at my age. But ever since the afternoon I lost control of myself at Mrs. Osmund's, I've been fighting a "gone" feeling in the pit of my stomach. I'm scared.

The next day I went back and apologized to Mrs. Osmund, and she said that if I'd come to get my job back she was sorry. She'd already hired her nephew who, besides delivering and such, would live right in the house with her and take care of the man's chores. I told her I was sorry for losing my temper, and couldn't I finish the cardboard signs to make up for what I'd destroyed. She said no, she'd decided not to have any weekend specials, but if I wanted to make some deliveries—just that one afternoon because her nephew wouldn't come for another day—I could help her out that way, and yes, she would give me a recommendation when I sought another job.

So after all my vows, there I was driving that panel truck one last time. How fitting, I told myself grimly, as I looked over the addresses on the deliveries I had to make. Longwood Hospital!

Then a thought struck me.

With my last pay check from Osmund's I bought a nice bowl of assorted small plants, plus a cute little cork man with popping eyes that I stuck in the middle of the plants. Just looking at his funny face made me laugh. Down in the basement I wrapped this in green waxed paper with great care. I attached a blank card. On the card I printed carefully—Lyle Abbot.

Now it's a little lighter. Outside the window the aspen leaves which have hung limp are beginning to flicker in even a hint of a breeze. The maple leaves, heavier, shake gently, and down the street I can hear the Johnsons' cocker barking. A small delivery truck is rattling along Mountain Pass. A squirrel on the roof sounds like an ox, and the woodpecker who is digging a home in a large oak knothole over our garage has begun excavating noisily.

I'd been working on my scrapbook of Hit-and-Runs.

Morbid? No, I don't think so. My scrapbook came about because I wanted to study the cases of pedestrians hit by cars, as printed in the newspapers. What happens to a driver who does not run? Is he held? Fined? Imprisoned? *What?*

Believe it or not, there are a fantastic number of hit-and-runs. In no time at all I was loaded with clippings which, you can be sure, I didn't want my family to find lying around. To preserve some order, I started gluing them in the back end of my last year's history notebook. I started at the back and worked forward. Quite by accident I worked out this system: on the left-hand page, stories about The Haunted Boy; on the right-hand facing page, all the other Hit-and-Runs I could find to clip.

A Longwood man, I read, *has been charged with manslaughter following what authorities said was a hit and run here Sunday.* Manslaughter. What did that mean: to be charged with manslaughter? I decided I must work the word into dinner table conversation, casually, and find out from my dad. I read on, *He was released on a $2,500 bond.* I shivered.

Here was another: *An 8-year-old south-side boy was injured Monday, police said, when an eastbound car sideswiped him on Maple Street and continued in an easterly direction. The boy was taken to Longwood Hospital where he was treated for bruises and released.*

Lucky boy. Treated—and released.

The next clipping held my attention a long time. It told of a little girl, six, who was fatally injured when she ran in front of a car near her home. The driver saw the girl standing on the curb and slowed down. She ran in front of his car, he said. He was not held.

"He was not held," I whispered half-aloud.

And here was another: *Authorities said Chris*

Anderson, 73, was walking along county route C at the edge of Soldiers Grove when struck and killed. The driver was not held.

The driver was not held. The newspaper didn't even print the driver's name.

Actually, as I sifted through my hoard of clippings, I could discover no clear-cut pattern of punishment for striking a person with your car. A 19-year-old youth, I read, whose auto struck and fatally injured a 54-year-old man May 17, was fined $50 Wednesday for imprudent speed. Imagine that! Causing a man to have a cerebral hemorrhage, and then being fined only $50.

Deep in thought, I tiptoed away from my pasting at the old dining table and wandered again to the attic window.

Down on our front lawn two robins were stalking about, cocking their heads, and plunging their beaks down for worms and grubs. There was a mistiness outside because it would yet be some time before the sun got high enough to chin itself on the heights in back of our house. Somebody besides me was up—I could smell coffee. But here at the window I couldn't tell whether it came up the flues from our kitchen, or was wafted on the breeze from the Cones' house.

"What are you doing up here so early?"

Startled, I spun around.

Eukie stood near the table, wrapped in her warm red-and-green checked wool robe. Eukie is always cold and even in the summer she wears socks to bed.

"What's all this?" she asked, fingering my papers on the table.

"Just junk," I said, moving swiftly to place my hand on the history notebook.

"Junk—I'll say!" she sniffed daintily, if a sniff can be dainty. "The stuff you collect. Gee, you're a magpie sort of person."

"And you . . . you're a—" I bit my tongue on the word *sneak* and my weeks at the flower shop came to my rescue. "You're a cactus person. You needle and you prick." Bird's-Nest Cactus. Red Pincushion. Bishop's-Cap. Devil's Cane. Boxing-glove Cactus. I'd no idea there were so many varieties before Mrs. Osmund hired me.

Eukie yawned noisily. "What's this?" she said, picking up my largest clipping, one which I hadn't pasted with the others because it didn't fit the categories. It was a news story that had fascinated me, an account of a penalty imposed on seven young traffic violators, plus a large picture of the grim youths standing with a judge and a medical examiner before an immense bed-sized sink.

Eukie read aloud, "Seven sober-faced teen-agers Wednesday stared at a corpse in the county morgue and a few minutes later vowed that in the future they would be more careful drivers. The youngsters visited the morgue as part of a program to combat juvenile traffic offenses." Eukie wriggled and scratched her cheek. "For heaven's sake!"

Now fully alert, she stared at me with her widespread eyes.

I sent my mind groping around hurriedly. "I . . . I thought one of those boys was—" My voice was rough. Bracing myself against the table, I whispered hoarsely, "I thought I'd played golf with him, but I hadn't."

Eukie dropped the clipping. "Why do you come up here so early? You haunt this attic."

There was that word! Haunt, haunt.

Hurriedly I used one of Eukie's tactics; I changed the subject of conversation from me to her. "Have you got your summer all planned?"

"You know I have. I'll be going to summer school and slaving in the drugstore." Her very blue eyes inspected me and all she could survey of the attic as if she were seeing us for the very first time. "I've got to plan ahead," she said, almost self-righteously. Then she added something that took my breath away. "After all, I'm not an heiress."

Dumbfounded, I stared at her. Then I giggled. "I only wish I had a dollar or two. I'd buy a new golf glove. What are you talking about, anyway, Eukie?"

"Why, the things your mother left you, Stupid. All that jewelry you inherited."

"Well, of course, my mother left me her jewelry, but it's not all *that* valuable. I mean, it doesn't make me an heiress."

"Oh, no? Well, if you ever tried to sell it, you'd

find out. Some of that jewelry you think is junk would bring you a small fortune."

It was Eukie's tone of voice, more than her actual words, and the expression on her face that startled me. *Eukie was jealous of me.* I hadn't known it before.

Suddenly it occurred to me that she knew a vast amount about the jewelry. It was a shock. Maybe she hadn't obeyed Mother's command to stay out of Marilla's private cupola!

I looked over to the second drawer in my desk: the postcards and envelopes, the paste and scissors, and the newspapers with LYLE ABBOT and with LONGWOOD HOSPITAL clipped from them. Did she know about those, too?

Eukie was staring at me with a brooding look.

What did she know?

And what would she do? And tell?

"You don't like me, do you?" I whispered.

She jerked her head around. "I've tried to," she blurted. "I've tried to *do* things for you. I've cooked chocolate recipes, I've knit sweaters for you, I've done—whatever I could think to do. They say a person likes somebody if she can do her favors. I've really tried . . . but—"

For a moment she looked as though she was going to cry, then she got hold of herself. She spun on her heel and, as if she couldn't get away from me fast enough, in her haste she half stumbled down the attic steps.

Chapter

: 15 :

The Employment Office of the Jones-Galen Manufacturing Company is a gray-painted, glass-blocked place, completely walled by cabinets, and decorated, you might say, with card files. Last week when I went for my interview, a man named Mr. Twinley took me to a small room furnished only with a long table and chair where I was instructed to fill out several pages of tests—all fairly easy for me because the questions were almost duplicates of aptitude tests we'd had in high school. I could have finished them in half the time allotted but I decided to go slow and be unusually neat, so when Mr. Twinley came for me I still hadn't completed the last two sections.

He acted as if this was unimportant. "We'll file these," he said, and then he began to talk about my golf.

Now, I felt, the real interview was starting.

He told me that Jones-Galen felt they had acquired a "real fine golf course," and they wanted a "real fine team" to represent their "real fine company." In honor of the founder and the first president of the corporation it would be known as the Galen Course, and because it was private it would play against the country club teams in the district matches. Naturally, right from the start they wanted a team in which Jones-Galen could take pride.

"Of course, we haven't had years of competition to build up a team like the other clubs." Mr. Twinley played with a pen, clicking the ballpoint in and out. He was a dark, gaunt, hollow-eyed man who made me think of either Ichabod Crane or a young Abraham Lincoln. "And because the membership of the Galen Course is limited strictly to company employees," he said, "it behooves us to employ a few who can really hit the little white ball."

I smiled. "That's what Lloyd said."

"Lloyd thinks pretty highly of you." And now he began to question me about my experience. How much did I practice? What was my handicap? Had I lowered it by many points lately? What was my lowest all-time score? What competition had I been up against? Was I best in match or in medal play? Was I a good pressure player? In short, just how much seasoning had I had?

He kept nodding his head as if my answers were the ones he wanted. He asked if I intended to go to college. All the years of my life I'd planned to continue right straight through school until I had earned my degree, so I started to say, "Oh, yes," but I caught hold of myself. My thoughts veered back to the memory of the fat envelopes addressed to Lyle Abbot.

I smiled weakly. "I would if I could, but there's the matter of money."

"There always is, isn't there? Well, you'll hear from us," Mr. Twinley told me. But all the way home, and all this week, I've worried about how indefinite his words were. Certainly, he promised me nothing!

I've been hanging around Lloyd's place whenever I can escape the house. But for the first time I'm not enjoying golf.

Now I *have* to be good at it. I have to practice. I have to spend hours blasting out of a sand trap. My back still aches from bending over the putting green.

And Seth seemed to have gone into hiding. Why didn't I see him around? Did going to Tech Institute need so much preparation?

At breakfast this morning Eukie said to Mother, "If you don't mind, I've asked Seth for dinner. Mrs. Cone has gone on a trip and Seth's tired of his own cooking."

With a clatter my spoon dropped to the floor. Again—Eukie and Seth. I bent down to pick up the spoon.

Mother made an occasion out of that dinner. You would have thought we were having the President of the United States to dinner instead of the boy next door. She stuffed and baked trout. She prepared a casserole of asparagus and little white onions in cheese sauce. She made popovers, and to top it all, both lemon and apple pie.

Seth, seated between Jimbo and me, was wearing a new white sport shirt. My, he looked handsome. You could see he was pleased. It's easy to relax at our dinner table. Manners aren't too, too exquisite—they can't be with Jimbo and Jeff around—and generally there's so much conversation with everyone fighting for a chance to talk that Dad has to act as the chairman and allot each one his minute or so.

Tonight was no exception. Mother started the first discussion when she mentioned she had seen a bluebird, right on our front porch in her fernery, and Dad said she must be mistaken; bluebirds are practically extinct around Longwood, and Mother said, for goodness sake, she surely knew a bluebird when she saw one—a statement which drew from Eukie the comment that she always had thought her mother was a little color-blind—at which point Jeff knocked over his glass of water.

While this was being mopped up, Dad turned to me and said, "Rilla, you haven't mentioned anything about college for a long time. Did you get your acceptance from City?"

"Yes, but . . ." My eyes clung to my hands which buttered and re-buttered my popover. "I'd rather work a year."

There was a chorus of "How come?" "That's a crazy idea, if I ever heard one" and from Mother a baffled protest. "You've worked hard, Marilla, and we want you to use your savings on yourself."

Impulsively I blurted, 'I haven't any savings. I *want* to work for a year."

Everyone looked at me with a shocked expression. I flared, "For heaven's sake, why do we have to discuss me at the dinner table?"

All this time Seth seemed to be concentrating on his food, yet I was aware of waves of consciousness passing between us. Probably trying to ease the situation, he asked, "Did you get the Jones-Galen job, Rilla?"

"I don't know."

My dad was not to be diverted. "You've been earning money. Where has it gone?"

Jimbo said, "I think she spends it on golf."

"I do not." I spread my hands. "Look at the blisters. I ought to buy a new glove—but . . ." I looked around the table. "Has anybody seen a leather glove with no fingertips around this house?"

Dad rubbed his chin. "How much do these gloves cost?"

"Under five dollars," I said hastily. "I—I really don't need another."

Dad said, "And golf balls?"

Seth again tried to help me. "Nobody hits such a long ball as Rilla, so when she's a little wild . . . But we always hunt for out-of-bounds balls."

If only somebody at the table would bring up

another subject! If only they would stop staring at me.

Dad said in a meditative voice, "There have been times when I thought I should make you give up golf."

I protested. "But if I get this job at Jones-Galen it will be only because of my golf."

My dad made a motion as if brushing back hair that was no longer there on his high forehead. "Well, if you do get the job, I think maybe Mother and I had better check more closely on where your salary—"

Thank heavens, at that moment the singing teakettle sang. The telephone rang. And Jimbo got caught in the act of buttering both sides of his bread.

Momentarily I was released from the spotlight.

Before it swung back to me the meal had ended. But for the rest of the evening Seth was uncommonly quiet. Even during a ping-pong game in our basement he seemed far away.

After he had gone, all I could think of was the silent, searching look in his eyes as he held my hand at the front door.

Chapter
: 16 :

That was a summer!

No need to tell how lonesome I was for Seth.

His first week away, he wrote me a long letter describing his dorm, the endless registration lines, the orientation affairs for the new students—and homesickness crept through between the lines.

The second week there came a short note; and now even the notes would be welcome.

Yes. I missed him.

I forgot to say I got the Jones-Galen job, but after the first week factory work has become such a terrific bore I can hardly bear it. I have to stand over a moving counter loaded with cans and, all day, all week, put a cover on each can as it moves past. If I rub my eyes, straighten my aching shoulders, or if I stop to use my handkerchief, a contingent of cans oozes by without covers—and there, I've boggled again.

Oh, for the good old days when Mrs. Osmund gave me something different to do every time she laid eyes on me!

A dreadful thing, to waken each morning absolutely loathing the day ahead of you. The only thing I look forward to is golf.

But even when I won my points for Jones-Galen in our first match with the Burning Bush Country Club, I felt depressed and got only a little lift when I saw my name in the *Ledger,* the area medalist for the day: *82—Marilla Marston, Galen.*

I felt boxed in by life. Dad had begun to keep track of my pay checks, so I couldn't go on sending money to Lyle Abbot. I couldn't seem to do anything to ease my situation.

One hot day, standing over the cans and thinking about everything under the sun except the covers I had to put on those cans, it occurred to me that perhaps Eukie might be correct. Maybe I did have something of value in my mother's jewelry. Maybe I could secretly sell some and raise money that way.

But how do you go about selling old jewelry? And to whom? How do you know what the value is? Who can you trust? And will a jeweler trust an 18-year-old girl, or will he get in touch with her parents about the jewelry?

I decided I'd watch the classified ads in the Sunday *Ledger.*

Maybe I could learn something without having to ask suspicious questions.

I could start with one ring—one diamond in an old-fashioned high-pronged gold circlet. If I made one sale smoothly, and without arousing any questions then . . . then . . .

"W-what?" I shouted over the noise in the immense Jones-Galen plant. "Oh—*that* can . . . I'm sorry, I'm sorry."

It was the third of July.

I was adding in my head as I swung off the bus at the Mountain Pass stop after work and walked toward home. "Thirty. Thirty-one. Thirty. And three in July." That made ninety-four days since April Fools' Day. Almost one hundred days after my hit-and-run.

I *must* be perfectly safe.

On the Fourth of July, I carried through a scheme which had tantalized me ever since I thought of it. Now that the *Ledger* no longer carried a running account of Lyle Abbot's condition, I had no way of knowing if he were making progress. I had no way of knowing if he were still in Longwood Hospital, or if he had been moved to a nursing home, or—well, I had no knowledge about him at all.

I dressed in my most feminine clothes, borrowed one of Eukie's pastel velvet bows for my hair, carried purse and gloves like a lady, and went to Longwood Hospital.

I sat in the lobby, as close to the Information Desk as possible, pretending I was waiting for someone, and listened.

Centered squarely before the elevators was the

reception desk, staffed, on this July Fourth only by a voluble redhead.

Less than half the chairs were filled. Trying to be inconspicuous, I selected one behind the big pillar closest to the desk where I could see little, but hear all.

With a faint careless smile I opened a magazine in my lap, bent over it blindly—and listened.

You have no idea how much you can learn about a person's life by eavesdropping! The privacies that people make public. The redhead's name was Mary, and Mary talked to a gray-haired lady as if every statement she made was of vast importance. Some people can do that: their manner makes their words seem important, no matter how trivial they are. And everyone listens to everything they say. On this Fourth of July Mary was getting used to her contact lenses. They *slayed* her! The visitors who tried to sneak by her desk without a permit *slayed* her! And having to work on a holiday *slayed* her!

"Yes, it is a quiet afternoon here," I heard her agree with the gray-haired lady. "Sure you can go. I can handle this alone."

I fidgeted, pinching my skirt into tiny tucks.

Why had I come? Whatever had given me the idea that I could learn anything this way?

The girl at the desk caught my eye. "You've been waiting a long time," she said politely.

I stood up. If she had noticed me, there was no point in trying to hide any longer. "I guess my friend isn't coming," I said lamely. "I might as well go."

But I couldn't walk out without learning anything. I'd counted on today. I tried to make my voice sound casual. "Isn't this the hospital where that newsboy, the one that the *Ledger* writes about so much . . . ?" my words ended in a swallow.

Now I had her complete attention. "Yes," she said, and again she thrust back her shoulders and sat stiffly alert. "Do you know him?"

"No, I've just read about him in a magazine," I said, suddenly suffused with a longing to be any place but here in Longwood Hospital. Why did she look at me like that?

"Good thing you're a girl," she said, reaching for a pencil and pad. "Want to give me your name, please?"

"Why?"

"The police want a record of everybody who asks about Lyle Abbot. If you were a young man I'd have to make an excuse to detain you."

"Give you my name? But just because I ask—" I looked about, somewhat wildly. "I'm only waiting here for a friend."

Don't panic, I told myself. I clasped my hands tightly around my white purse. It was ridiculous, but I was filled with the same terror that had possessed me the night of the accident when I waited in this same hospital—and waited, and waited.

The red-haired clerk had started to write on a pad. She looked up, waiting for me to speak again.

And then I did exactly what I had done once before in Longwood Hospital.

I ran.

"Marilla dear, come down for supper now. I've kept it warm for you." Mother's head appeared as she stopped halfway up the attic stairs. In the dusk her face looked pale and her worried brows were drawn together over her eyes.

I cleared my throat. "I'm not hungry."

"You've been rocking an hour. Come down and drink some fruit juice if you don't want to eat. You'll make yourself sick."

I am sick, I yearned to tell her. Taking my handkerchief, I wiped it across my eyes.

But why should I make Mother worry? "I'll come . . . in a short while." My voice blurred. "Just give me a few moments more up here."

"All right, Marilla," she said doubtfully.

Chapter

: 17 :

The first weekend in August.

Saturday, nearly dusk—and I waited in my bedroom for it to be dark enough to retrieve the luxurious red golf bag that I had won today at the Jones-Galen Company picnic. I had it hidden under the lilac grove behind our garage. I wanted to sneak it up the back stairs to an attic hiding place.

Dad was watching my salary closely, and he still thought I was spending too much on golf. I'd have to think of something to tell him before payday. If I had only known there was an entry fee that would be deducted from my salary, I would not have played.

Kneeling by my window, I watched the birds, restless this month and flocking together. Already our big elm tree looked tired and rusty and had begun to shed old leaves. In the distance a mourning dove called plaintively.

I concentrated on thinking up a good story to tell Dad about the golf bag.

Suddenly I put my head against the sharp windowsill. I couldn't remember ever knowingly lying to him. But these days I was sneaking, I was lying —talk about character deterioration!

Nothing eventful happened at Jones-Galen those next few weeks. Nothing eventful would *ever* happen on that boring job.

Then, to my surprise, I became quite a heroine. I played for Jones-Galen in the Metropolitan Annual, a three-day tournament for the low handicap players in the county, and I had the good luck to come in third. In my co-workers' eyes, for a young girl to come in third the very first time she entered the Metro was a triumph. Mr. Twinley, too, is pleased. He called me into his office for an interview today and it amused me, the way he discussed how *we* had played in *our* initial bid for the Metro.

I saw my opportunity. As if it were just occurring to me, I said, "I've enjoyed the Galen Course so much that I . . . well, I almost wish I could go on working here so that I wouldn't have to give up this course."

Mr. Twinley pushed up his black-rimmed glasses and let them ride on his eyebrows where they looked like goggles. "You mean you're not going to college, Rilla?"

"I would like to work for a year. And then I'll go on to college." I was hoping he would not ask me why.

Mr. Twinley doodled some strange figures on his note pad. Then he scratched the back of his head. "Well," he said thoughtfully. After a time he added, "In a plant this size we can generally find room for one more person."

When I went home I was resolved to discuss a year of work with Dad. I would settle this and not worry any more. It turned out that he didn't come home for dinner because he was shorthanded at the drugstore. After drying the dishes I felt restless, so I started out the front door, not exactly knowing what I was going to do, maybe just walk. I wished, as I often had wished lately, that I had a close girl friend. But I had never made friends easily, and since Seth left I'd felt lost for companionship.

There was always a crowd from Kennedy at the Old Plum Grove lodge. You didn't need a date to join in the fun. But a crowd wasn't what I wanted.

I thought I was walking aimlessly, but after a time I found myself meandering near Mrs. Osmund's shop. A long time passed while I inspected her window display. Fussy, I thought, a hodgepodge. Painted enameled kitchenware mingled with fancy hankies, plants, jewelry, and greeting cards. There was too much. If only I could get my hands on that display; I'd clean it out.

I felt homesick for Mrs. Osmund and her store. And I knew I was itching to see what was parked by her back door these days.

A new panel truck.

A white one, nicely lettered. How nice for Mrs. Osmund, I thought. And how nice for Rilla! Now the *weapon* had disappeared.

Then I caught my breath. In the far corner of her back yard stood the old truck.

Why was it still standing there? Why hadn't she traded it in for the new one? Yes, it was practically worthless; maybe it wasn't of enough value to bother with—but why was it still standing in her back yard?

I wondered if the key was in it. I stood staring at it. Wild schemes darted through my mind. It would be easy to drive it to Old Plum Park and set the gears so that it might slide down the bank into the river.

After what seemed like a century I drew a long breath and started toward home.

Mountain Pass was deserted. A firefly lit on the rolled-up sleeve of my blouse. It sat there blinking like a Christmas light, as if it were trying to cheer me.

The downstairs of our house was deserted. Wandering out to the kitchen, I found a chocolate cookie and was pouring a glass of milk when the telephone rang. Because I receive few calls, generally I don't rush to answer. I leave that to Eukie and the boys. After pouring the milk I put the bottle back in the refrigerator, listened to the ringing, and waited for a rush of footsteps upstairs. But all was quiet.

Swallowing some milk, I picked up the receiver. "Marston residence," I said, as Mother insists that we do. "Rilla speaking."

Nobody answered. After a couple more "hellos" I hung up. Wrong number, I thought. But it seemed queer, and I began to feel uneasy.

Chapter
: 18 :

Tonight dinner started out innocently enough. We were having a complete oven meal; that's one of Mother's fetishes, she can't stand wasting one square inch of space if she has 350 degrees in the oven, so we had baked *everything:* meat loaf, potatoes, escalloped corn, orange-flavored baking powder biscuits, and—pure luxury—a warm gingerbread cake. If she could, she would have perked the coffee in the oven.

"September the first," Mother said, moving the butter plate away from Jimbo so there would be some left for the others. "Where has the summer gone? I still haven't trimmed the back hedge that I was going to do in June. If only you boys could do it, but you'd cut off exactly what I wanted to save."

"We sure would," Jimbo agreed, glad to get out of a job that easily.

"I like living next to a wild hillside," Mother continued. In our family she is generally the one who does most of the talking at the beginning of a meal because, having tasted and sampled in the kitchen, she isn't as famished as we are, and from past history she knows that after the rest of the Marstons have taken the edge off their hunger she may not get a chance to get a word in. "But the wildness is moving right down into our yard. We've got to stop it. The next thing you know we'll be cultivating poison ivy."

Jimbo snickered. "We could put up a sidewalk stand and sell it. I know two or three people I'd like as customers for poison ivy."

Mother gave him a look. Stirring her iced tea, she said, "Eukie, why were you trying on every outfit you own today? Have you a date tonight?"

It was unusual for Eukie to look embarrassed. "Maybe, maybe not," she said briefly.

Sipping, and looking over her glass, Mother said, "Could I ask with whom?"

Eukie shrugged. "You could, but I'd rather you wouldn't." Now she had the entire family interested.

Imagine the commotion when she said flippantly, "I expect to see Seth. He's been home several days."

"He's home?" I faltered. "Is he sick?"

Jimbo yelled, "Did he flunk out?"

"It doesn't figure," Eukie said thoughtfully, "and Seth isn't doing much talking."

Seth home several days, and I didn't know about it? I tried not to let my face show what I was feeling. If only I could hide under the table for a moment!

I jabbed my fork into my gingerbread cake, but

I couldn't eat another bite. I jumped up from the table. "I'm busy, too, tonight," I said. "Let's get these dishes out of the way."

With a curious inflection in her voice, Mother said, "Rilla, I'll help you with the dishes."

Our kitchen is the least attractive room in the house in spite of all Mother's efforts to improve it. She can't do much, largely because in the days when homes like the Johanson home were designed, the architect stuck the kitchen away in a cell-like corner with a back entry blocking light and vision on one side, stairways on another, and a pantry on the third. By means of lemon sunshine-colored paint and a shelf of African violets in the high-ledged window, Mother has made the room as cheerful as possible, but only thousands of dollars, she says, can do to it what it needs, so let's make the best of it.

We do, by staying out of the kitchen as much as possible.

"Oh dear," Mother murmured, scraping the dishes I carried to the sink, "not enough meat left for sandwiches tomorrow."

Making other comments, she tried to coax me into conversation, but when she saw I wouldn't cooperate, she said, "I want to tell you something, Rilla, something I should probably have mentioned years ago."

"Years ago?"

"Yes. It struck me again tonight that Eukie always wants things that *you* have."

"I haven't thought much about it," I said slowly, twisting the towel inside a glass.

Mother's face was grave and her voice was solemn. "When I married your father, you know, Eukie was my only baby. I guess I'd spoiled her, poor little thing! *Her* father died before she was born. So of course she was jealous when your father and I were married and presented her with a new baby sister. I didn't notice this at first—I was too busy trying to make friends with the shy little girl that *you* were."

"You probably paid too much attention to me."

"I probably did. And that may excuse her some; but now, just because she's gotten away with so many selfish little things all these years, she thinks she can get away with bigger ones. And we mustn't let her—for her sake as well as yours. Rilla, your father and I both know how much Seth likes you. And Eukie knows it, too. But she can't resist needling you."

Mother was splattering water unnecessarily, and her voice was low and somehow heartbreaking. It told both how much she loved Eukie, and how disappointed she was in her.

I felt a great need to be comforting. Patting her shoulder, I whispered, "Don't worry. Please don't worry, Mom."

A smile started way back in her eyes, worked its way forward, and then it reached her lips. "That does me good—your calling me Mom."

After I'd hung the two damp towels on the back porch line to dry, I climbed to the attic and sank into my rocker. Seth was home—and I hadn't known it. How many days had he been in Longwood? And what was I doing up in this attic? Why wasn't I running next door to say "Hi"? Why wasn't he running over to say "Hi" to me?

After a time the attic had just the opposite effect on me that it usually did: tonight it gave me claustrophobia. When it grew completely dark I wandered down onto our front porch and sat in the swing. I'd wait there, I decided, until it was time for Eukie's date. When Seth came I'd say "Hi" casually. I wouldn't let him see that I was worried. "Glad you're home," I'd say. "I missed you." No—I wouldn't say that. Perhaps I could suggest a game of golf. Sure, that's it. I'd invite him to be my guest on the Galen Course.

The sky was particularly dark tonight. No stars pricked the blackness. Occasionally there was twittering of birds in the trees. Was that lightning in the distance?

Down the street a clock chimed, and between the sidewalk and the curb a rabbit ran, unaware of me. As I sat there, a mild but steady wind began to blow, picking up strength gradually. Soon it was gusting along Mountain Pass, causing whirlpools of dry leaves in the street. A storm was coming.

I sat there pretending everything was all right, but every now and then I looked over toward Seth's house for a sign of some activity.

The wind began to chill me. Well, I couldn't sit here but neither could I go into our house with its peaceful shining lights. I had a need for the dark so I skulked across our front lawn, then hesitated: should I go east or west on Mountain Pass?

Suppose it hadn't been Eukie who had announced that Seth was home? Suppose it had been Jimbo spilling out his daily accumulation of odds and ends?

Right now, or even an hour ago, I'd have been banging on the Cone door, whistling to let him know it was me, and demanding: "What's wrong, good friend?" Not with those words, of course, but Seth was my good friend.

Slowly I mounted the steps to the Cone doorway. Lightly I touched the bell.

The door swung open and tiny Mrs. Cone peered out, then smiled at me. "Rilla, come in." And as she stood aside and waved for me to precede her, she said in a stage whisper, "Seth's home and we're so worried about him. He says he's quitting school, and he's in such a strange mood. Maybe you can pull him out of it. We don't know what to do!"

I whispered, too. "Quit school!"

"He says he can't concentrate. Can't study at all—so why should he stay and flunk out?" Her hand fiddled with a blue and silver clip she was wearing on the collar of her white blouse. "He promised he'll go back, but not this quarter."

Now she pushed me into the living room. "We

had to work overtime at the office tonight so we're having a late meal," she said as Seth and Mr. Cone arose. Side by side they stood as they greeted me, and never before had I realized how much they looked alike.

Seth seemed both surprised and glad to see me. "How are you, Rilla?" he asked.

Before I had a chance to answer, Mrs. Cone chirped on. "The more efficient I become at the office, the more there seems to do, and I never catch up." She giggled abruptly, amused at the expression on my face.

"I didn't know you were working!" I said.

"She is," Mr. Cone said. "In my office. And she's a top-notch secretary already." He threw the newspaper he was holding onto a small table, and spoke with great geniality. "I don't know what I'd do without her."

Nobody asked me to, but I sat down abruptly.

Mrs. Cone was laughing softly. "Before Seth left we had a family conference. My men decided that I had too much time on my hands, which wasn't good for me, whereas my husband was overworked trying to make a living." She shook her head. "I live with two tyrants."

Mr. Cone tamped tobacco into his pipe. "She's surprised all of us," he said decisively. And Rilla could see the look of pride on his face.

My eyes swiveled from Mr. Cone to his wife, and back again. Here was no tragedy. They may once have had problems, but if anybody had ever defeated trouble, this pair had.

Then why—*why* the forlorn expression on Seth's face?

To keep from meeting his eyes, I let my own wander about the room. Magazines spilled from a wrought-iron rack; old golf balls lay on the carpet in a far corner, and a putter was propped against fireplace logs.

A big bowl of fruit and nuts overflowed onto the man-sized coffee table, and two emptied cups of coffee awaited a trip to the kitchen sink.

I put my fingers to my brow and rubbed. Obviously Seth's unhappiness couldn't have anything to do with his parents.

Suddenly a most unwelcome thought jabbed through me. Eukie! It must be because of Eukie. And with that quirk of human nature that makes a person torture himself, I said, "She's ready and waiting for you."

Seth said gruffly, "Waiting for me? Who?"

"Don't you have a date?"

"Not that I know of."

Now I was really puzzled. To cover my confusion, I babbled, "I'm pretty well set at Jones-Galen, Seth. It's a boring job but a nice pay check. I . . . I was kind of wishing you'd have a game with me at Galen Course—that is, if you feel up to golf."

There was a curious inflection in Seth's voice. "I'll think about it, Rilla."

I faltered, "Don't you l-like Tech Institute?"

"It's all right."

I brushed a nervous hand over my long hair. Seth's face looked gray. "What's wrong, Seth?" I wanted to ask, but didn't dare. Suddenly I began to steel myself against a feeling of danger.

Uneasily my eyes darted around the room. Always the Cone family has had what they call their "junk" basket sitting on the lamp table by the fireplace. It's an immense fruit basket, a catch-all, and now, right on top, was something I hadn't seen around for three years. There was the makeup kit I'd lost under the front seat of the Cone car the night we weren't supposed to use it.

I must have looked surprised.

"Oh, that's yours." Mrs. Cone sprang to her feet. "I meant to return it to you when Seth told me . . ." And she thrust the kit in my hand as if glad to get rid of it.

I sat there looking at it blankly when Seth said, "Confession is good for the soul, Rilla."

What did he mean? A spasm of nervousness made me shiver. Just then an enormous arrow of lightning split the sky. A boom of thunder shook the house. I jumped to my feet. I could use the storm as an excuse to escape.

I was conscious of Seth's eyes watching me as I hurried to the front door. "See you later," I called with false gaiety.

Huge raindops slapped the dust as I ran out into the storm. I ran past our house and down Mountain Pass with the wind blasting my face and tangling my hair. I was sobbing.

I thought I heard footsteps behind me and ran faster.

Chapter
: 19 :

In my panic I was almost directionless, yet, subconsciously, I was aiming for the place where I'd always found comfort.

When I reached Lloyd's shanty by the deserted golf range, I was out of breath and I had a sharp, stabbing pain in my side.

In the dark I slammed into the Coke machine. When the lightning flashed I must have looked like a witch with my streaming hair. Ever since the foggy night of April the first I had been running in my imagination, hunting for some kind of safety. I couldn't run any more.

I stumbled on the graveled pathway and it was then that the footsteps caught up to me. I felt someone clutching my shoulders so hard it hurt.

"Let me go! Let me go!" I screamed.

Seth's voice was harsh in my ears. "Stop it, Rilla. You're hysterical." I was hauled around and shaken until my teeth chattered. "I tell you, stop it or I'll slap you."

I shrieked, "What are you doing? Spying on me?"

I couldn't see Seth's face but there was such pain in his voice as I'd never heard before. "Oh, Rilla!"

"Why did you come home?"

"To help you—if I could."

"You left school because of me?"

"I—I couldn't study. I thought my parents were still having difficulties . . . but they aren't, thank goodness . . . and then, knowing you were in some kind of trouble—well—"

"You've got a funny way of helping me," I accused. "You come home, and don't even let me know about it."

"I tried to call you." His voice came out of the dark, troubled, severely shaken. "I telephoned when I thought you'd be alone but when I heard you answer—well, I didn't know what to say."

"You mean you were the person who phoned last night?"

In the rain I stood, feeling shaky, leaning against a post. It seemed so unfair. All the punishment I'd taken; all the punishment I'd given myself.

I heard him make a peculiar noise that seemed to stick in his throat. After a time I heard a muffled, "Rilla, I just can't bear what you're going through."

I took a step nearer him, then stopped. Defeated, I asked, "How did you *know?*"

His voice was gentle. "You told me. That day at the zoo."

"But you didn't believe me!"

"Not then. But later, especially during dinner at your house the night before I left for college, when you said you had no savings at all, and it was all so mysterious. I know you don't spend much on golf. Then I put two and two together. When I went away I didn't know what was going to happen to you and . . . well, when I tried to study, all I could see on the page was you, so—" He broke off, then added somberly, "so I came home. But I can't tell anybody the reason I came."

"You mean you aren't going to tell anyone about me?"

"No."

I had known he wouldn't, without asking. I could trust Seth. He wouldn't tell. But suddenly I knew *I* must. I couldn't stand the deception—the agony—any longer. But how? How could I? "What'll I do, Seth?" I moaned.

He must have sat down. I could hear the creak of the old wooden bench. His voice sounded tired. "You have to decide, Rilla."

The wind was whipping against my legs, plastering my hair back from my forehead, spattering my face with rain. Absently I brushed my wet face with my wet fingers. When the lightning flashed I could see Seth hunched over. He made no sound.

I slumped down on the bench beside him. I began to cry. "Will you go to the police with me, Seth?"

I could barely hear his words. "If that's what you want."

I seemed to want him to tell me what to do. "Don't you think I should?"

"*You* have to decide, Rilla."

I sighed heavily. "I've decided." I added, with an effort, "Ever since April Fools' Day life's been miserable."

We sat there for a time, oblivious of the drenching rain. After a time Seth's arm reached out and he drew my head into the warm hollow between his chin and his shoulder. He didn't say anything. He just held me there. And then I cried, I really cried.

"I'd better tell my parents first," I said at last.

He brushed my dripping hair from my face. "I'll go with you."

My voice broke. "I don't mind the police as much as them."

I could feel his cheek against my forehead. He needed a shave.

"Oh, Seth, now I can ask about the newsboy. It will be such a relief to say openly, how is Lyle Abbot? I never knew, Seth, I never knew what was happening to him, and the newspapers stopped telling me."

I closed my eyes and clenched my hands. I thought, if only I might stay here all night, Seth holding me, if only I could stay here for the rest of my life.

Chapter

: 20 :

The living room seemed full of people. Dad sat with his shoes off, his bow tie hanging, and his head lowered over the financial page of the evening *Ledger*. Mother was bent over her interminable mending, sewing a button on one of the boys' faded trousers. Sprawled on the floor, Jeff and Jimbo were working a crossword puzzle.

In her new autumn plaid skirt and a melon-colored sweater, Eukie filed her nails.

It seemed as if one hundred eyes stared at Seth and me as we came out of the gloom of the entry hall into the lighted room. Their expressions changed from surprise to apprehension when they took in our wan-faced and bedraggled appearances.

"What in the world—?" Mother began, then stopped short.

"I'm in trouble," I gasped, my hand clutching Seth's for courage.

Nobody spoke. Everyone remained absolutely motionless, staring.

I glanced from Dad's wide, strong but gentle

hands holding the newspaper, to Mother's dark head, just beginning to gray, to beaver-toothed Jimbo and freckled Jeff, and to Eukie who, last night, had done all my personal ironing without even mentioning it to me, in one of those peculiar temperamental quirks of hers that leave me baffled. Never had I loved my family so much.

I yearned to spare them unhappiness but there was no evading. I said, almost curtly, "I'm the person who hit the newsboy in Longwood Hospital. I . . . I'm the one who ran away."

Momentarily the silence held. Then Eukie's voice cried incredulously, "You're crazy, Rilla. That was a *boy* who did it."

"Tell us about it," Dad said. "How did it happen?"

"With Mrs. Osmund's truck," I answered. "That's why I have no money. I've been sending it all to the boy—to Lyle Abbot."

Dad looked stunned.

"I'm not going to let this accident be an expense to you, Dad," I blurted. "I'm going to pay every cent of the cost myself. That's why I want to work before going to college. And I'm going to sell my mother's jewelry—"

"And what will *that* get you?" he interrupted brusquely.

I stammered, "Isn't it v-valuable?"

"If it were, do you think I'd allow it to gather dust in an attic drawer! It was—just your mother's, that's all."

Slowly, as if he'd caught a severe case of arthritis while he was sitting there, Dad pushed himself up out of his chair. "Well, it's a bad night," he said quietly, "but let's go to the police and get this over."

Mother dropped her mending on the floor. "I'll go with you."

Our police station shares a red-brick building with the Fire Department and with a branch of the Longwood library. An officer was sitting at the desk behind the counter, listening with a telephone clamped over his head.

"A minute, please," he said, indicating that Mother and Dad, Seth and I, were to take chairs.

Sitting there, I shivered and realized that we shouldn't have been in such a rush to get here; Seth and I should have stopped to change our wet clothes.

Mother smiled at me, and her hand covered mine.

Now the officer turned to us. He was a large man with intensely blue eyes. "What can I do for you?"

Dad stood up. "We've come about the Abbot case—the newsboy that was hit. I just learned tonight who hit him," he said, nodding to where I was sitting beside Seth.

Momentarily the officer did not say anything, but he made an *O* with his mouth. "Oddly, I'm not surprised," he said thoughtfully. "All along we've thought there'd be a confession in this particular case. It had all the aspects. We've been waiting." Then, standing, he said, "Just a minute," and he went into a back room.

When he returned, he was carrying something in his hand. It looked like a dry, brittle maple leaf. Putting my hands to my cheeks, I felt the heat rise there. I knew I was flushing.

The next moment my mouth opened with astonishment. Because the officer, throwing my lost dried-out leather golf glove on the counter, said to *Seth,* "Here! Try this on for size."

A startled gasp came from each of us.

The officer, mistaking our surprise, said, "We found this quite near the wrecked bike but we had absolutely no way of connecting it with the accident. It might have been there for days. All we could do was trace it, and Lloyd admitted he'd sold a number like this—among others to Seth Cone, and also one to your daughter, Mr. Marston.

"We've studied your father's car when he hasn't known about it," the officer continued to Seth, "but that passed inspection."

"Look, you've made a mistake," my father interrupted, jumping to his feet. "It was my daughter who had the accident."

"A *girl* hit the newsboy?" The officer's brows drew together and his mouth twisted with disbelief. "I don't get this at all. Why in the world would the nurse describe a boy?"

"I may have looked like one that night," I told

him unhappily. "I used to wear my hair real short until the accident. I was wearing jeans and an old sweater. The nurse really didn't look at me, she was so busy. I didn't know where I'd lost my glove," I said slowly. "You see, I carried it in my pocket all the time because I never knew when I'd be grabbing a stick, or a broom, or an old club—anything with which I could practice the rhythm of my golf swing. I don't know when I first missed it."

The officer went into the back room and we could hear the sliding of a drawer and the conversation. The Abbot case had broken, we heard. Then he returned carrying a file that he was leafing through, and another policeman came behind him. These two were Officer Ford and Officer Pinea.

They talked to each other in voices just a degree above a whisper. "No, the *girl,*" Officer Ford said. He studied a paper in the file he was carrying. "Were you the young lady who visited Longwood Hospital on the Fourth of July?" he asked me.

I nodded. "I didn't know how to find out what had happened to the boy," I said miserably. "The newspapers stopped telling how he was."

Officer Ford looked at me kindly. "We felt we were dealing with a sensitive person who would *need* to confess. As a matter of fact, the Abbot boy had left the hospital when you inquired."

I looked down at my clenched hands, too stricken to talk.

Then I had to describe all about that night. A

tape recorder registered my words, and Dad and Mother and Seth listened as avidly as the two policemen while, shutting my eyes, I told about the fog and about missing my turn-off on Mountain Pass, and about how I had to follow the painted center line in the road, and that I didn't see the boy on the bike, did not know what I had hit until I stopped to investigate.

The two policemen asked many questions. Sometimes they seemed to advance and retreat with questions, asking the same ones so often that it almost seemed as if they weren't listening to my answers, but I guess they were just making sure that I had the details of the accident absolutely correct.

Anyway, when they shut off the tape recorder, they finally seemed to believe it was actually me, a girl, who had hit Lyle Abbot.

About this time both Seth and I began sneezing.

So the rest of the formalities were carried through in a hurry, with both the policemen talking about the foul weather outside and with me in a daze. Now I let the others do the talking. I'd said all I wanted to say.

Dad took over for me.

Hugging myself, I sat hunched in the smallest ball I could make of myself, as close to Seth as possible for warmth except that he wasn't any warmer than I was.

"What do you think they'll do to me?" I whispered.

"They're releasing you to your father."

"What does that mean?"

"It means your father signs a bond for you, I guess, promising your presence in court when necessary—or something like that."

He sneezed explosively.

"Don't catch a cold," I begged. "I want you to go back to college right away. I don't want you to miss another day. I can't be responsible for—for anything else." I added, "I wish I could go to school too. Oh, Seth, you can't imagine how boring my job is. But I'm glad I have it."

But did I have it now? Probably I would not after Galen-Jones found out about me.

I looked up. "We will call for you at eight o'clock tomorrow morning," Officer Ford was saying. "We'll take you to the Abbot home and we would like you to come with us, too," he said to Seth, who nodded. "We're scheduling this interview as early as possible in the morning, before the *Ledger* breaks the story."

So now I would have to face Lyle Abbot.

Chapter
: 21 :

I had often wondered what the row houses on Cobb Road were like inside. Today I found out.

Officer Ford rang the bell and the door swung open as if the woman had been waiting, hand on knob. Immediately I had a contrasting impression —Mrs. Abbot was so wide and the house so narrow. She was about forty, but looked older because of her bulk. She had a colorless, very round face and brown hair with a strand of gray springing from each temple. The house, which shared side walls with the houses on each side, seemed like a long hallway with furniture on each side and a pathway in the middle from the front windows to the back windows.

"Good morning, Mrs. Abbot," said Officer Ford, and in a low voice introduced Officer Pinea, Seth and me. "You didn't tell him?"

"You asked me not to, so I couldn't make him dress for breakfast because he's gotten the habit of eating in his robe."

The policeman nodded. "We won't be here long."

She waved us toward the back of the house.

The kitchen was just a small space directly in back of the stairway.

At the table a young boy stared at us from over his bowl of oatmeal. How could I ever have thought he reminded me of Jimbo? He had very red hair and large freckles. He was terribly thin and it made his eyes seem too large for his pointed face. He was wearing a greenish plaid robe that looked as if it might have been cut down from an adult size. One thing he had in common with Jimbo, I noted: he overbuttered his toast.

Silently he studied the crowd of us in the doorway.

"Good morning, Lyle," said Officer Ford. "We've finally found the person who's been sending you those envelopes of money." What a nice way for him to put it, I thought humbly.

The boy lifted his brows. Now, for the first time, I saw a scar along the side of his forehead. I wondered about it.

"We're asking you to identify the person who brought you to the hospital," said the uniformed man. "Is that person in this kitchen now?"

For a long moment Lyle Abbot was quiet.

His eyes swiveled from one to the other officer, finally settled on Seth. "I don't know if he's the one," he said, shaking his head. "I don't know, I didn't see him." Suddenly he blurted, grinning at

Seth, "Gee, thanks for the new bike. You should see the swell one I bought. The *Ledger* has kept my job open and I'm ready to start peddling as soon as Mom gives the word."

The two officers looked at each other. They grinned, vindicated. Lyle Abbot had made the same mistake they had. No wonder they had requested Seth to come along this morning.

To be truthful, Lyle Abbot seemed a bit annoyed when he learned I was the guilty one. A *girl.* He didn't believe it; he simply didn't believe it. And having thanked Seth for the bike, he wasn't going to thank me.

"I . . . I'm sorry," I said.

"Forget it," he shrugged, and at that moment he really did remind me of Jimbo. He returned to his oatmeal.

I gave his mother a sidelong glance. "Will he . . . is he completely all right?"

Her eyes looked large and they were ringed with shadows. "We thought there'd have to be plastic surgery because his forehead seemed paralyzed. Did you know," she said, dipping her head as she pointed first to her eyebrow and then above it to a spot near her hairline, "that there are seventy-nine muscles from here to here—and all of them were severed!"

Horrified, I clapped my hand to my mouth.

"But yesterday we had good news. The muscles have healed and are working." She shook her head as if she couldn't believe it. "The doctor says he thinks sanding will do the job on the scar."

"Oh—fine," I said, not knowing anything about plastic surgery, or sanding—but just glad that she was glad.

"He'll be going to school this week," she said. "Our neighbor, who used to be a teacher, has been tutoring him. He's all caught up with what he missed last spring."

"That . . . that's wonderful." Suddenly I wanted to cry. We couldn't leave this house fast enough for me. I was very tired.

"The trouble I could have saved myself months ago," I said to Seth, after the police car had deposited us in front of home.

We stood there, Seth and I, in front of the old Johanson place which meant so much to me. A pocket of cool air in a warm breeze hit me. I looked up and down Mountain Pass and I was overcome by the same feeling of love for all that was near and dear to me that I'd had last night when I faced my family, about to confess.

Pensively I looked down at my fingertips. Now I had a police record. Now the district attorney would decide what ought to be done with Marilla Marston. So far, today seemed pretty much like yesterday. So far, I was still prowling the dark, cluttered alley called regret.

From the hillside came the sound of a complaining crow. The wind, which had worked so hard last night, was resting today. I saw that while I'd been occupied with other matters a couple of trees had gotten an early start on their fall wardrobe, changing from summer's green to rust-red.

I felt Seth's knuckles prodding my chin upward. I saw his face through a misty blur. Now he'd be leaving; he could catch a bus in less than an hour, and that's what I wanted—Seth back in college—yet I hated to have him go.

His face was grave. "I'll be coming home soon between quarters. Be a good girl until then—promise?" And when I nodded, he said, "Our first date will be a game on your Galen Course. I'm going to beat the tar out of you."

"That's what you think," I said shakily.

As he had done once before he ran a soft finger around the outline of my mouth. "I'll be seeing you, Rilla," and he leaned over and kissed me.

"G-Goodbye," I tried to say, but I couldn't bear to actually see him go so I spun on my heel, slammed into our house, and sped up the curving staircase. Straight for my cupola I aimed; straight for the rocking chair that comforts me when I need to work off emotion too big for me to handle.

So . . . if you live in Longwood and are a daily reader of the *Ledger* you'll be reading about me again. You'll be able to finish that mystery which began on a fog-shrouded April evening when a paper boy was hit by a car while making late deliveries: I won't be *X* to you any longer. I'll be Marilla Marston. It's going to be hard to face you —but it's going to be easier than running!

About the Author

Hope Dahle Jordan was born at Mount Horeb, Wisconsin. She now lives in Elm Grove and loves the state so much that she never wants to live anywhere else. She began her creative writing while working for a New York advertising firm. "I was bored and set myself a goal that in three years I would have something published. And I did." Her short stories have appeared in a dozen or more American magazines—including *Seventeen, Ladies' Home Journal, Catholic Home Journal* and *Christian Herald*—and also in Canada, England, Norway, Italy, Sweden, New Guinea and Australia.